HERZONE

crocus

c r o c u s

HERZONE

Fantasy Short Stories by Women

First published in 1991 by Crocus

Crocus books are published by
Commonword Ltd,
Cheetwood House,
21 Newton Street
Manchester M1 1FZ.

Commonword gratefully acknowledges financial assistance from the Association of Greater Manchester Authorities, North West Arts Association and Manchester City Council.

Produced by Wordsmith, Progress Centre, Charlton Place,
Manchester M12 6HS.
Printed by Manchester Free Press, Jersey Street, Manchester M4.

British Library Cataloguing in Publication Data
Herzone: fantasy short stories by women
   823.08766089287

   ISBN 0 946745 80 3

Contents

Introduction

Writing fantasy is often a liberating experience for women. In escaping the constraints of more realist approaches to fiction, fantasy allows women writers to explore other worlds or ways of being, as well as a whole gamut of moods from the serious to the whimsical. And as we prepare for the second millennium its visionary and speculative qualities have an added edge...

Fantasy certainly isn't escapist, neither is it always about escape in the literal sense. Often it subverts reality, taking a different approach to current issues or difficulties. We see this in stories such as 'Home to Mother' and 'Reflections in the Afternoon'. Fantasy can be provocative. It can make us ask questions about the present, look afresh at the world around us. And it can be mind-expanding, opening up new vistas on life and experience. The two stories 'In the Bleak Midwinter' and 'The Curse of Brandverd' give opposing views of future worlds, the first stark and grim, the second more optimistic, more woman-centred. Fantasy can be about revisiting and reviewing older forms of storytelling. Myths and fairytales are reworked in 'The Thirteenth Blessing' and 'Medusa My Mother'. Fantasy can also be fun – and a lighter tone is found in the whimsical speculations of 'A Day Out' and 'Ill Met By Moonlight'.

We think that *Herzone* is well named. It is a place where women have explored their dreams, fears and fantasies, both for here and now, and for the future.

Finally, we would like to thank the members of the editing group for their invaluable help in making the final selection of stories for *Herzone*. They were: Norma Brown, Jane Broughton and Di Williams.

Helen Windrath
Commonword

In the Bleak Midwinter

E. M. Kkoullas

Summer was over. The cold nights were coming and great black clouds threw torrents of rain to drum and splash on the roof. She had decided that they would have to make a journey to the market to stock up, as she had been rummaging through the stores and had found something unaccountably and obviously missing.

'The rats,' Akeel said, 'they get hungry this time of year.'

She hated the rats, the small subtle noises they made in the night scratching somewhere in the darkened house and the feeling that rooted her in horrible fascination when, as a traveller in distant lands comes across the unknown, she would find their tracks in the snow outside.

'They must have found a secret way in.'

'Hmmm.' Akeel was busy thinking.

'I'll go and see if I can find it, then we'd better be off to market. They say it's going to be a bad winter.'

'Fine.' And that was that.

Searching carefully she found the hole in the wall just above floor level and sealed it off, noting the gnawed edges with distaste. Maybe if it was very cold they would die.

When she returned to the kitchen, wiping her hands nervously, Akeel was already changing his gear and, recognizing the signs of departure, she hurried to do likewise. She pulled on her hat and let her mind wander over the list of things they needed; that was hoping people had made it through the rains. All too soon they would turn to freezing slush, then one morning she would wake up to find the whole world transformed in whiteness. By that time, though, they should be safe in the knowledge that they were prepared, with enough to eat until the arrival of spring.

It was very crowded at the market that day. Everyone was stocking up for the long dark nights and days ahead and several times she feared that she would lose sight of Akeel in the crush, or fall and be trampled. The babble of voices confused and frightened her – she could never get used to so many people in one place, not after the silence of the open, empty countryside.

She thought of the rats again and shuddered. No matter how strongly built a house was, they would get in eventually. Her dad had shown her how to kill them with a stout club, after smoking them out. Poison would not work. The thing that she hated most was waking up to find them in the room. She remembered the way their eyes glittered. Akeel would just have to check everything when he put up the barricades, that was all.

Their wagon was soon filled with the grey-green plants whose fleshy stalks were their main diet. Some roots and dried fruit were added as a treat. It would be a long hard haul back home, with the wheels sticking in the mud as like as not. They could not afford to wait for the freezing. Nor could they forget anything. Salt and a little dried meat from the trapping gangs who followed the wolf rats all summer. It was expensive – trapping was a dangerous business – and furthermore could only be done at that time of year when the beasts were fat and comparatively slow. Come winter they grew lean, alert and very hungry. Once the barricades went up nobody ever went outside their compounds. Usually families banded together in villages, but she and Akeel lived with just each other for company. She did not mind. Akeel spent most of the time working, on what she was never quite sure. He said it was to do with the way things were before the Long Freeze, when everything that had lived before had died or become strangely changed. Akeel also said that people had caused the Freeze, but she did not understand that. How could people affect the weather?

She stared at the leathery salted hunks of meat in their barrel. She had seen a wolf rat once, dead beside the road. She had hoped that a trapper had killed it, but her dad said no, it had died of old age. See the grey hairs? In summer it would be allowed to rot in peace – any that fell in winter would be eaten immediately by the starving pack. The huge body was already in an advanced state of putrefaction, but she remembered the curved incisors, yellowed and blunted, in her dreams. These she could understand perfectly, although she sometimes thought Akeel never would. If she wasn't there to remind him to eat, he always forgot.

Akeel returned later, much later, to where she was standing guarding the wagon. People would take if there was nobody claiming the goods and there to prove it. She could tell that he had been after something; he was always interested in any bits and pieces that the trappers brought in. This time he had an object tucked under his arm, wrapped in cloth round and round so she couldn't tell what it was. She knew better than to ask.

Without a word they each took a shaft and collar and began the long three-day trek home. The roads were difficult to pass, cratered with deep pot-holes into which the unwary might stumble and drown, not knowing the depth. In winter they were deadly to old or injured wolf rats, which often fell through the snow and ice to lie trapped until death or spring, and with this last, men came to put an end to them.

The three days on the road were punctuated by nights spent in safety at friendly villages on the way. Nobody would refuse shelter at night to the weary traveller. On the third day, soaked by the steadily falling rain, they sighted the compound, its heavy gates locked against the rats. These would have to be opened to enable the wagon to be pulled through. They crossed the makeshift bridge over the ditch carefully, then Akeel tramped round to the low side door, opened it, and unbarred the gates from the inside. The wagon, its precious load protected by layers and layers of thick material, was hauled inside. All that had to be done now was the dismantling of the bridge, then the gates would be shut until spring. The side door would be barred and bolted, the heavy spikes would be fastened in place on top of the high walls and more would be planted at the wall's foot. The surrounding ditch also carried a fringe of spikes, though any wolf rat attempting to cross would fall into the freezing water beneath the layer of snow and drown. All they had to do was sit it out behind their defences and wait until the danger was over.

Two days later she came across Akeel in the kitchen, usually her province as he spent most of his time in his study. He was standing at the sink brushing something gently. Peeping over his shoulder (with difficulty, he was far taller than she) she saw with a start that it was a skull. An animal skull, she corrected herself. Wolf rat? Their skulls were sold in the market as deterrents to their living brethren. No, the great incisors were missing, indeed the teeth were different entirely though sharply pointed and clearly intended for meat.

'What is it?'

Akeel seemed in a better mood than usual.

'The skull of an animal that lived before the Long Freeze.'

She took a few minutes to digest this information.

'What sort of animal?'

He frowned, absently.

'A dog. One of the trappers found it on a riverbank. It took enough to persuade him to part with it.'

She sighed.

'How much this time?' She had thought she was used to his mania for curios, but she hated wasting good cloth on such rubbish. Cloth which she had spent a lot of time weaving.

'One of those thick rugs.'

She fumed inwardly. That thick rug had taken her nearly a week to weave, not to mention the hours she had spent collecting and spinning the woodfibres, then dyeing the material afterwards. She could not remember when Akeel had last made something for market. All that for a lump of bone. It wasn't even a whole skull; the lower jaw had gone and some of the teeth though she supposed that if the animal had been old it might have lost them naturally. Still, it had been a bad bargain.

Akeel finished working loose the last pieces of encrusted mud, then set the skull on a shelf to dry.

'And don't touch it,' he added, disappearing off into his study, presumably for the rest of the day. Messing about with his old junk when he should have been out there putting up the fortifications. With another, deeper sigh, she pulled on her hat and coat, picked up as many stakes as she could carry from their cupboard and staggered across the compound. It took her a few minutes to get them all to the top of the wall. Dropping her clinking burden she paused to gaze out into the greyness beyond. The woods lay silent under an iron sky. The rain fell in rods. The small furry animals which could occasionally be spotted nosing through the brief summer grasses had disappeared into their winter burrows, fattened by a season's hard grazing. If they were lucky, they would remain safe until the ground thawed and they could emerge, blinking, into the light.If they were not,they would make a tasty meal for a wolf rat.

A raindrop touched her cheek. Was it her imagination, or did it already have a taste of frost? She shivered and began to work methodically until most of the cold had left her. For the next hour, the effort of jamming the spikes into their rusty grips occupied her full attention. It was only as she forced the last one into position that she became aware of a sudden movement to her right, among the outbuildings.

Turning sharply, she just caught sight of a tail vanishing behind the fuel shed. Her brain automatically sprang into gear. What was it? It could not be a wolf rat. Nor had it looked to be a small rat, their tails were thin and hairless. For a sickening moment she pictured herself trapped on the wall, unable to get help or call to Akeel.

A minute dragged by. There were no more sudden movements in the stillness of the yard, or unidentified animals, so she decided to risk the dash into the house. The rain was growing steadily heavier and she suspected that the freeze was starting to set itself in motion. By tomorrow morning the season would be suddenly changed. She would awake in the night, huddled under the blankets and listen to the world solidifying around her with brittle crackings.

She took a deep breath and ran.

Once inside the safety of the house she fled to Akeel's study.

'What's going on?' he demanded, glaring at her.

'There's something in the compound, I saw its tail.'

Akeel grabbed his cloak and a heavy club, then together they searched the house and compound.

Nothing.

Wet and tired they returned, the panic having given way to anger on his part, bewilderment on hers.

'I did see something!' she insisted.

'A trick of the light.'

'No!'

He scowled at her, his giant's face ugly in the half-light.

'You'll be seeing your old man next, I suppose, walking through the gates with his head in his hands.'

She bit her lip and glared back as he laughed derisively and returned to his room.

'I hate you,' she whispered, while her inner self recoiled in horror, 'I hate you.'

The reference to her father, three years dead, had killed any sympathy or gratitude she had still felt for Akeel. The debt she owed him for sheltering her after her family had died had been paid long since by her hard work. Left to Akeel if the wolf rats hadn't killed them, starvation would certainly have done so. Now the cold was here and the neglected barricades would just have to stand as they were.

That night, a pall of ice formed over the compound and the encircling woods, followed by the first flurries of snow. The siege was on.

Akeel spent more time locked away, emerging only for meals. She still had no idea of his work and found she cared even less. Yet she was disturbed. The sounds that crept around the house at night were probably the rats, or the wind snapping icicles from the roof. Twice she thought she heard a howling from the yard and, on rising and opening the shutter, seen a dark shape slipping away, but in the morning these night terrors faded. She checked for tracks but found nothing.

She did not mention it to Akeel. The winter wore on.

Solitude was not hard to bear for one such as she, unused to having people constantly around her, but during the dark evenings alone she became aware of a feeling of foreboding creeping around the compound. It was nothing she could name, just a worry in the night, a presence. A spirit abroad? It was possible. Winter was the time, according to the elders, when the lost ghosts came to lonely compounds wailing, crying, or simply waiting in silence for the occupants to despair. Then more ghosts would move on to the next place and so on. She didn't know whether to believe or laugh, as Akeel did, though his laughter was bitter. He was growing worse – she feared he had an illness. Secretive he had always been, but never like this and it made her afraid.

Then, one quiet day in midwinter, the wolf rats came.

There was a small pack of them, about fifteen in all. The winter had hit them hard; they were thin, vicious and intensely frustrated at having so much food so nearly obtainable. She watched them from her window as they waited patiently outside, their breath twisting white in the frozen air. They were wondering what to do to save their lives, she knew that. Their squealing yelps pierced the silence as they discussed the problem. When no immediate solution was reached, and death by starvation imminent, they killed one of their number and ate. In a few minutes, the writhing frenzied heap of fur parted, leaving nothing but an irregular patch of bloody snow and some tattered scraps of skin to be quarrelled over. This done, their hot yellow eyes fixed on the compound, the council recommenced.

She ran to Akeel's study.

'Akeel!' She pounded on the door with her fists. 'Akeel the wolf rats are here! Akeel? Open the door, please?'

There was no answer to her frantic calls, so at last she left the house and went to the study window. The shutters were open. Through the dim, frosted glass she could see a shadow, long and thin, crouching on the floor. Akeel? She blinked and it was gone. Then her eye fell on a hanging shape swaying gently.

She reeled away, her back pressing against the hard coldness of the wall. Outside, the yelping increased.

Slowly, her breathing evened and she dared open her eyes. It had begun to snow again, and the light feathery touches on her face served to bring her back to her situation. Her instincts told her to check on the wolf rats, but a sharp cracking, a splash, and a shrill scream informed her that one had dared the ditch. This would temporarily distract the others' attention as they would try to retrieve the body. The real danger would come if they became light enough for the ice to support their weight.

She was alone, but she knew what to do. There were still two and a half months of winter left, but she would have enough supplies – they would be safe enough from the rats inside their barrels. Her mind worked rapidly, calculating. Hopefully the wolf rats would lose heart and go after easier prey.

But Akeel? What had she seen? Curiosity overcame her now the crisis was past. Stiffly, she went into the house, removed her snowy coat, then made her way to Akeel's study. The door was solid, barring her way. She would have to hack it through with an axe. It took her an hour, during which the only sounds were the thump of the metal and her own breathing. Night was drawing in; she fetched a lamp, then continued to chop at the splintering wood. By the time it fell, she ached badly, but she would not give up.

Once inside she paused, lifting the lamp by its wooden handle to get a better view. Akeel had never let her inside, so she was unsure of its contents. For a second her gaze rested on the now still figure, then it travelled around the rest of the room. Death had never frightened her. Why be afraid of something inescapable?

The room was lined with shelves on which stood Akeel's collection. Twisted metal shapes, boxes and other assorted oddities reflected blackly in the glow of the lamp. As she turned, the dog skull leapt out of the dark, its empty sockets in sharp contrast to the polished bone around them. In a corner near the window, a table stood cluttered with papers and wooden markers. Remembering how Akeel had once shown her how to make marks with them, she moved to look. A single sheet lay uppermost, then she saw that it was many sheets fastened together. They were covered with black markings. She studied the top layer with interest.

'I have attempted once more to get out of this god-forsaken place, to get home. I cannot. The formula will not work and I cannot tell why. Twenty years of hell are enough and now I have lost hope. I had thought that the skull would help me concentrate in working myself back, but all I could achieve was the summoning of part of the dog. I hear it howling at night in the yard. It crouches in the corner as I write. I know I have become worse than useless in maintaining this place. It should last out until spring, but no longer. Nor am I any use to my sole companion of the last three years. Geared for survival as all these people are she could never understand. I cannot even pronounce her name. Now there is no hope of warning anyone – inevitability has finally caught up with me. This is how things are. I can only hope that Man in his resourcefulness – and these pathetic creatures are indisputably men – will some day find a way out. Meanwhile, I dream at night. Of rats, always of rats. I have no antidote left. My hair is starting to fall out and I vomit frequently. I am not adapted to this poisonous environment. I would prefer to die quickly than to linger in madness.

'The wolf rats have come, but they are the least of my

worries. Nobody will know what I have been through. I can only conclude that the experiment, and therefore I, are both abandoned. I don't even know why I am writing this.'

Eventually she gave up trying to decipher the marks. She recognised only two groups of them, alone at the bottom, the marks that meant Akeel. She traced them carefully with a finger.

Achille Foulon.

She smiled. He had left something of himself after all and, although she would never know exactly what, she felt comforted. She had enough to do until spring, and now there would be plenty of food too. When the freeze ended she would move to a village and settle there. They would be glad of some more hands.

The room was bitterly cold, the fire having long died out; by morning the body would be frozen hard. On her way out, she stopped for a second, gazing at the strangely deformed figure. Poor Akeel! He should never have laughed at the lost ghosts. Had she not heard them with her own ears? Shaking her head, she hurried into the kitchen to find a sharp knife and some salt.

Ill Met By Moonlight

Sylvia Christie

Miss Smithers – 'my friends call me Midge, but my name is Myfanwy' – was no longer young, and had never been beautiful. She had few friends to call her Midge, being of a shy and retiring nature. But she had one outstanding attraction. Since her recent spectacular win on the pools she was very, very rich. This brought her little satisfaction.

'I really don't know what to do for the best,' she confided to the expensive ear of her solicitor, Mr Abernethy, the senior partner in the firm which, having handled all her father's meagre business, seemed almost affronted by her sudden affluence.

Mr Abernethy regarded her with some exasperation. Plump, untidy, bespectacled, a tweed skirt dipping in unexpected places, ringless hands clasped in maidenly supplication – where had the woman been living?

'Well, my dear –' he hesitated. 'You have a substantial fortune. Now, I can recommend all sorts of useful investments, and I'm sure you will be sensible. But –' he paused again, for he was a kindly man at heart. 'Have you thought of actually spending any of it?'

'Spending it? I couldn't spend it!' Miss Smithers was scandalized. 'Just think of what Father would have said if I squandered all that money!'

'Surely he wouldn't have objected to you enjoying yourself for a little while?'

Miss Smithers wasn't at all sure about that. Father, a tyrannical figure in white whiskers and black suit, had had a rooted objection to anyone enjoying themselves.

'What I was going to suggest was a holiday,' Mr Abernethy went on. 'What about a couple of weeks in a nice hotel? Have you ever been abroad?'

She admitted that she had not.

'My late wife and I,' said Mr Abernethy, a reminiscent light in his eye, 'spent many happy vacations in Greece. The classical ruins, you know. Athens. Delphi. Enchanting...' He sighed.

Miss Smithers perked up.

'Classical ruins? Father was interested in the Greeks, of course. Quite a number of his sermons mention them – not their religion, of course, Mr Abernethy, just their high principles and wonderful civilization.'

Mr Abernethy nodded, beaming.

That's the kind of thing!' he said. 'You'll enjoy it! I'll tell you what – why don't you go along to Travelbest in the High Street? They'll fix you up!' It would be best, he thought, not to mention that his nephew Vincent worked there; the lad was not his cup of tea, but could probably do with the commission to support his lifestyle. He hoped Miss Smithers would not notice the strong family likeness.

Shyly, she thanked him, and leaving her uncomfortable million in his hands, left the office.

Before she could change her mind, she walked down the High Street. Travelbest was a suave, sophisticated establishment, and once inside, a suave, sophisticated young man took her in hand. Under the smooth face and athletic build, he reminded her of someone – who could it be? – but she was far too shy to comment on it. Once it had become evident that money was really no object, in less time than she could ever have imagined, she was in Greece.

The resort was small and intimate, and furnished with an idyllic golden beach fringed with dramatic bluffs of red and yellow rock, carved by the caresses of the brilliant sea. The hotel was not too obtrusive, and her room was luxurious. Trips to various ruins were part of the holiday, and she enjoyed them all, wandering entranced among the ancient stones under her broad straw hat like an animated mushroom. In the towns, she bought souvenirs; in the villages, sun lotion, films, and flip-flops for the beach. It was all wonderful, and her only sadness was that she was alone.

It was therefore with pleasure overcoming her usual shyness that she discovered, towards the end of her first week, the suave, sophisticated young man from Travelbest at the next table in the hotel. He smiled at her, and, greatly daring, she smiled back.

'Do you mind if I join you?' he said. She blushed.

'Please do.'

He sat down opposite her.

'We've met before,' he said, still smiling. 'I don't suppose you remember...'

'Oh, I do!' she said. 'At the travel agents.' She blushed more, wondering if it was too forward of her to have shown she remembered him. But he seemed happy to chat about the classical tours and the surrounding delights of the area. Really, he was most interesting – at least as interesting, she thought, as the travel brochures. This was not surprising, as that was where he had gleaned his information. Miss Smithers spent a delightful evening, laughing at his stories, lifting her ringless hands in horror or wonder, and before the baklava was stickily disposed of, he was Vincent and she was Midge, and there seemed to be no reason in the world why they should not stroll together under the brilliance of the new moon.

'Before we go,' she said, 'do let me show you the little souvenir I bought today.'

He waited on the terrace. What has the old fool bought, he thought. Some vulgar trash, those frightful plaster casts made for the tourists. It's obviously easy enough to separate her from her money.

Presently, breathless and smiling, she came back, and handed him a small package.

'I do think it's rather nice,' she said. 'What do you think?'

He whistled. Gleaming softly, the tiny form of Artemis of the Crescent Moon was a delicate blend of artistry and dream. Made of heavy silver, exquisitely detailed, the goddess stood naked and graceful, and the crescent moon on her miniature forehead sparkled with small diamonds.

'You must have paid a fortune!' said Vincent. Her brow clouded.

'Oh well,' she said. 'It's only money... But I did think she was rather nice.'

Hastily he diverted her. It would not do to dwell on her money...

'She's beautiful,' he said heartily. 'Beautiful. What wonderful taste! Do you know, there's a legend about Artemis of the Crescent Moon here?'

She clasped her hands.

'A legend? No, I didn't know. How lovely – I love legends!'

She wrapped the little figure up and put it in her capacious handbag, and they began to stroll towards the beach.

'Out there –' he pointed. 'Out there – do you see the channel between the rocks? It's called the channel of Artemis. The local girls – the maidens, that is – they used to swim the channel, naked, on the night of the crescent moon. And if they were truly virgins, Artemis rewarded them with a vision of their future husbands.'

'Oh!' Her eyes, or at least her glasses, shone rapturously in the moonlight; the crescent moon was reflected in them, twice. 'What a lovely story! But – don't they do it any more? I wonder why not?'

'Can't get the virgins,' he managed to stop himself replying.

She became pensive, and turned towards the hotel. He thought of trying to pursue her into her room, but remembered in time that there were more nights in which he could press home his advantage. Something about her manner made him hesitate; she seemed preoccupied as he said goodnight, pressing her hand meaningfully.

Vincent went into his own room and poured himself a nightcap from his expensive little flask; it was nearly empty. He sat on the bed, thinking hard. He must be cautious; she was shy and easy to frighten off. At the same time, he must get a move on; the state of his hip-flask reflected the state of his bank balance, and being sacked from Travelbest last week had been a blow; he only hoped the little discrepancies in the books had been covered up adequately when he departed.

A sound from along the corridor alerted him, and he peered out of his door to see Miss Smithers retreating towards the stairs. She carried a bathing towel and was wrapped in a voluminous robe.

'The old fool,' he muttered. 'I bet she's off to try out the legend!'

Quickly, he slipped into his trunks and followed her. The channel, which he had examined earlier while she mooned over her ruins, led to the open sea. If he were to climb round the far side of the rocks, then surely – he chuckled – surely at the end of her swim, Miss Smithers would be granted a tantalizing glimpse of her future mate! What a good idea, he thought. That should convince her! Good old Artemis, giving me a head start!

Ahead of him, he could see the clumsy splashing in the channel which signalled Miss Smithers' progress. There was just time. He climbed precariously along the rocks that shielded him from her sight. This side of the outcrop was abrupt; he swore silently as the jagged edges cut into shins and soles; he must hurry, but he must be silent; he almost panicked, for she must be nearly there by now. He began to climb up and over, to meet her at the end.

He was almost at the top of the last rock when his foot slipped. He grasped at the rocks with clawing hands, desperately seeking a reliable hold. Straining upwards, he was able – just – to reach the top of the cliff. He began to haul himself up, kicking at the rock to secure a toe-hold. Suddenly, a sharp pain crushed his grasping fingers and made him cry out.

Above him, looking down from the height of the rock, was a silver figure. She was naked; her body gleamed in the moonlight, and the crescent moon on her forehead sparkled as her heel ground his bleeding fingers into the rock. As he fell, his face contorted by pain and fear, he saw her smile.

Miss Smithers, plodding back to the hotel, was perfectly happy.

'Artemis, Queen of the Night, my thanks to you,' she murmured to the moon, now sinking slowly towards the silent hills. How truly wonderful, she thought. She looked forward to telling dear Vincent in the morning how, when she had reached the end of the channel and clambered painfully up the rocks, she had indeed seen a vision. She smiled, remembering how the vision had faded, falling away from her towards the sea with a mysterious cry; but how even through the shining steel-rimmed glasses clouded with salt water she had distinctly seen the face of old Mr Abernethy.

Home to Mother

Alison Chisholm

I could tell Derek was in a filthy mood by the way he slammed the door. I smelt his cigar before he came into the kitchen. He dropped his briefcase in the middle of the floor.

'Good Lord, aren't you ready yet?'

I was becoming used to this sort of greeting.

'Ready? of course I'm ready. You're late.'

'M25,' he grunted. 'And I hope you don't mean you're coming to the Westons' like that.'

I glanced down, knowing Derek didn't like what he saw but past trying to please him.

'You look as though you're wearing camouflage. And those shoes. For crying out loud, Sarah, you're coming to have dinner with one of my colleagues, you're not going to put in half an hour on your precious garden.'

I bit my lip. It was no use telling him what I thought of his opinions, or of his colleagues. It would only start another argument.

I took a deep breath and said, 'I always feel good in green. You used to say it suited me.'

He looked at me, really looked at me for the first time in weeks. I hardly caught his words, for he turned away as he spoke.

'It suited you when you had long hair, like corn. The way you wear it now, all short and spiky, it looks more like stubble.'

The remark was nasty enough on the surface, but there was a trace of regret in his voice. I remembered how he used to stroke my hair when we were first married, how he would run his hands though it, and tell me how pretty it was.

'I'll tell you what, I won't change the dress but I'll put the war-paint on,' I conceded.

I shuddered at the sticky taste of the lipstick. Mascara felt heavy on my eyes. At least he had not insisted over the shoes, I thought, as I searched through the drawer for some nail varnish. The flat brown slip-ons were not glamorous, and his jibe was well-founded. I had worn them for gardening in the past. But my feet had been sore for a couple of weeks now. Even a short walk made them burn and sting.

Derek had poured himself a large whisky when I came downstairs again, and he downed it in one gulp.

'I'll drive,' I said. 'You'll be past the limit before we get to the table.'

He shrugged but he made no complaint. I never really liked driving his big car, the steering was heavy for me; but he was doing enough by poisoning his system without risking his licence. Besides, I've always preferred drinking water to alcohol, and if I said I was driving, the most hospitable hostess could hardly insist on ladling out the gin and tonic.

The Westons welcomed us with the condescending air they always have. If only Derek could see through it.

We ate roast beef. It was a large joint, and Howard carved at the table. He was almost slavering as he cut the slices and placed three, still bleeding at the centre, on each plate. I heaped vegetables on top of mine so I could not see the livid colour.

I focused on the conversation to avoid thinking about the beef.

'How's your son getting on at Oxford?' I asked.

There was a short silence, and then Howard spoke rapidly.

'He's no longer there. He left to take a job in industry. Computers. Doing well at it, too.'

Derek made some silly remark about my ineptitude with machinery, and they all laughed.

I tried to be friendly and relaxed, I really did; but it clearly had not worked. Derek started before I'd driven out of the path.

'Why are you always so damned rude to the people who matter?' he demanded. 'You're distant, you hardly speak, except to mention that no-good son of theirs. Didn't you know he'd been sent down? And then you left half your food...'

'I didn't mean to be rude,' I said wearily, trying to concentrate on the road through the pall of rain. 'I had no idea about the boy. And I'm sorry, I'm just not keen on meat any more, and when it's not properly cooked...'

'Don't be ridiculous, the meal was perfect,' he snapped. 'All this vegetarian business is just a fad, a sop to the conservation brigade.'

I let him go on, let him vent all his resentments on me. I knew I should feel sorry for him, for his frustration when promotions passed him by, for his knowledge that he was incapable of fathering the son he wanted. All I could think of was the pain throbbing in my feet, the claustrophobic confines of the car, the stale smell of cigars.

At least he had drunk enough to be asleep by the time I dried myself after my bath. Even with his eyes closed he had an air of discontentment and sheer bad temper. It had stopped raining. I opened the window.

The freshness of the air almost made me cry. The natural calling of the night was a balm to my bruised spirits. My feet still hurt.

Derek had started to snore. It was not a loud noise, and at one time, years ago, I had found it reassuring. Now it seemed to fill the room, squeezing out the air. I could scarcely breathe. I flung myself onto the landing and half fell down the stairs.

I was out in the garden almost before I realized where I was going. I ran across the damp grass, letting it bathe the pain away. I slipped through the gate into the tiny orchard. The apple trees stretched wide their branches towards me.

I dug with my bare hands, pulled the grass, exposed the network of roots. I stood naked in the hole I had made, paddling my feet in the soil, feeling myself slip into my rightful place, feeling at one with the trees and ecstatically happy.

I opened my arms and reached up. The moon touched my skin with silver, and at once a grey moth settled on my hand. A barn owl brushed past me, dusting my hair with its wing.

The pulsing of the earth penetrated my feet and surged its sap up my veins. This was it, this was living. This was my element, not the world of noise and smoke, of ugly people doing ugly things, of eating and moving and pain.

I settled myself deeper into the moist loam. I could feel something wriggling around my feet, some worm or insect. I welcomed it, sending messages through all my nerves to beckon towards me everything pure, and natural, and so, so very beautiful.

The one blot that still corrupted my mind began to fade. Derek receded until he was no more than a distant, ugly memory. I had come home to the only mother I could ever need; and the loving embrace of the earth made me whole.

The Knowledge

Pat Winslow

To most people I am an ordinary household brick. Only my friends and family know me for who I really am. Number nineteen, serial x. Programmed to – but never mind that. You wanted to know how I came to be here. If you come closer I'll tell you. But you'll have to put your hands on the glass first. I'm not used to shouting through this barrier yet. There. That's better. I can see you more clearly now.

Now, where was I? Ah, yes, I remember. The day I first came to Earth. I see you don't believe me, my friend. Well, stay a while. It'll all come clear, I promise.

The day I landed it was foul. Not what I'd been led to expect at all. No rain, no sun, nothing. Just bald, white nothing. And all the earth was hard. It was the year of the First Great Drought, only people didn't call it that then. Your people preferred to believe it was caused by sun spots, or something equally ridiculous. Solar activity and disturbed wind patterns. That was the commonest reason given. No one believed it, of course. But by then it was almost too late to do anything anyway.

Enter number nineteen, serial x. Destined – or so I hoped rather naively in those days – to change the world. Imagine my disgust at finding myself lying amongst a heap of rotting animal carcasses that human beings were feeding off. It wasn't so much the smell that appalled me, though that was bad, I'll admit. Rather, it was the way they were all grunting and snatching from each other as if they'd lost the art of communication. It was as though it had been starved out of them.

At first no one saw me. I lay there for several weeks, in fact. Quite inert. I only respond to human touch, you see. A hand. A foot walking across my broad face. A stumble followed by a cut knee. It doesn't matter. It's all the same to me. I'm nothing without human contact. Even this sort. That's why they put me here. Out of people's reach. They think they're nice and safe as long as I'm behind this glass wall. The label says I'm just a modern artefact. An early example of twenty-first century house-building materials. The first everlasting brick. Shatter-proof, salt and wind-proof, and – as if it mattered any more – damp-proof. But there are those who know otherwise.

Listen. The curator goes for her lunch at one o'clock. There's a change-over then. Mr Drabble comes on. He likes to check everything's in its place. Go and stand over there by the plaster cast Pershings and when he's settled down to read his paper, come back and I'll tell you the rest.

Who found me first? It was a little girl with a shaved head. I remember her exactly. Some boy was taunting her with a piece of piping. I think it must have been the exhaust from an old car. They were lying about everywhere in those days. Anyway, she spotted me and picked me up to throw me at him. Imagine my surprise. I hadn't even learnt how to send out signals at that stage. She must have done it of her own volition. Before I knew what was happening, I was whizzing through the hot air after him and then there was a tremendous impact, and the next thing I knew was that he was lying sprawled out in all directions with me on top of him. And she – well, she was just sort of standing there mesmerized. He was so much bigger than her, you see.

Dead? Yes, of course he was. Quite dead. I'd made sure of that. If you'd seen what I'd seen over those weeks, you'd have done the same thing yourself. Sometimes it was pipes. Other times his fists. They all did it. Women and girls were fair game, you see.

After that I went everywhere with her. We grew up together, so to speak. I was only in my infancy too, you understand, though you'll appreciate our infancy is considerably more advanced than yours.

I don't think she realized the possibility of our joint power until much later on. For a while, she just thought of me as a means of self-defence. And after that, I suppose, I was regarded as a talisman. A sort of good luck object. It wasn't until I accidentally fell into the hands of her grandmother that she started to question what, or even who, I was.

What happened? Oh, nothing particularly spectacular. It was the usual scenario. Man breaks into decaying flat with a crowbar, steals some food and water, and then tries to make off with it. His mistake was that he turned round and saw the grandmother watching him. If he hadn't lunged at her, I wouldn't have had to hit him at all. As it was, she got to me before the girl did and hurled me right from where she was sitting in her wheelchair. The electricity in the room was really quite astounding. Our three minds seemed to have come together just at the right point. You should have seen their faces afterwards, though. There was utter disbelief on the girl's, and something close to amusement on the grandmother's. We'd all three tasted the knowledge, but only I felt secure with it. I was, after all, a brick with a mission.

Nothing much happened after that. The grandmother never went out, the cable on the estate's lift having rotted away several years before that incident. Occasionally, I went out with the girl, though. Mostly when she was scavenging for food or work. They still had a thing called benefits in those days, but not many people qualified for them. She used to have to queue up for hours outside the relevant kiosks with her grandmother's cards. Red for bread, blue for fruit tablets, and green for vegetables. She fed them in like one does for money and a silver door would open up with her week's ration inside. I don't know how she paid for the water because she never seemed to have any money. Her grandmother was fond of saying that there was someone on their side in local government who kept their pipes open free of charge. I don't know whether that was true, but certainly there were a lot of break-ins from outside the area. Not everyone had water.

I remember a funeral several years later. It took place just after the Great Manchester Food Riot. It was one of the worst things I'd ever seen. The girl – or rather, woman now – was striding down the street with me bouncing in a bag against her thigh. She'd been for a job interview, and had struck lucky this time, so we were both feeling happy and in rather high spirits. Then she turned the corner, and instinctively I knew something was wrong. I felt her hand reach down and grab me and when she brought me out something strange happened to both of us. It was as if all the power we'd had suddenly drained away. There in front of us was a long procession of shiny black cars surrounded by the State Police. They must have sensed trouble coming because their rifles were already loaded and aimed at the thronging crowd around them. Someone from the back shouted 'Let's get the rich fucking bastards!' and immediately the police opened fire. There was no warning.

I couldn't see much in the general panic, but I could hear the screams of people as they fell to the ground riddled with acid shot. This time, though, the crowd didn't retreat like they usually did. The mood grew angrier. We tried to escape via one of the side streets but found our way barred by more State Police. The woman pressed herself back against an old shop doorway that was full of newspapers and stinking of cat piss, and together we watched as the police charged past us, armed with machine guns this time. What happened next was hideous.

The crowd's anger had grown to such an extent that they were in total disregard of the police who, try as they may, could not contain them any longer. People knew they were going to die anyway. It was just a question of how. We saw a couple, a man and a woman, dragging one of the mourners in front of us and then stop. They began ripping his fine clothes off him as fast as they could, and then, not seeming to notice the money that was tumbling out of one of his pockets, they proceeded to devour him bit by bit.

I say the power had left us but at that point we felt it return even stronger than it had been before. It was as if we both knew in that moment that we'd been born to do something big. That's the only way I can describe it. We went home that afternoon and found her grandmother weeping in her neighbour's arms. Someone had finally cut off the water supply.

No. Don't take your hands away from me now. There's more to tell. What's that? Mr Drabble's eyeing you suspiciously? Well go over and talk to him, then. Nicely, mind. Tell him you're interested in that catalytic converter over there. He'll be glad to explain it to you. He likes to show off a bit. Then come back tomorrow when Mrs Price is on. It'll be safer for us. Ten o'clock prompt. I'll be waiting for you. Ha ha. Very funny. I'm hardly likely to be going anywhere in this thing, am I?

The woman's name was Cookie. Look. What is this obsession with names? Why can't you just be what you are? Well, remember her then. Her skin was the colour of oak and she was six years old when she first came to me. No. I don't know where she is now. I never saw her after they took me away. Do you want to hear the rest or not?

Her grandmother made her call a meeting that night. Only a handful of people came. Most of the others were either too frightened or apathetic to bother. Their immediate task, they decided, was to restore the water supply. But first they had to find out where the underground reservoir was. Obviously there were no plans available to the general public with the water being in such short supply, but Cookie's grandmother had an idea. She'd seen someone dowse once. People used to do it when she was a little girl, she said. She told them how to take a fork of hazel and hold it in their hands, and then when the end tipped up towards them, that was when they'd know they were standing over water. It was hoped they'd be able to follow the pipeline out from the flats under the cover of darkness. Of course, they had two things on their side in those days. One was that there were still a few trees around and the other was that the local government hadn't bothered to repair or replace any of the street lighting for the past two decades.

Finding it was easy. They were very competent women, I must say, and I suppose it was no accident that most of them had bricks of their own. Anyway, to cut a long story short, they managed to slip past the armed guards, who were both as high as kites on something or other, and gain access to the vaults below. It was there that they found all the various ground plans for the region and, stuffing them inside their shirts, they crawled on their hands and knees down one of the ventilation shafts to wait for the night shift to return.

Murder is an easy thing to commit when you're desperate, and when security is lax. I don't know how many people we killed that night, but most of us had to agree afterwards that it was worth it when we found out that the water was being stockpiled and siphoned off for the sole use of business and government officials. When Cookie and the others consulted the ground plans in the distribution office that morning, they found all the major pipelines into the estates and turned them back on. They turned off all the supply that had been going to all the most privileged sections of society.

It was during the attack that followed that I first discovered the facts of life. Not yours. Mine. Most of the other women had been either shot or taken away and their bricks went with them, probably to be thrown away on some heap somewhere. God knows there were enough used car depots in those days. But Cookie – well, that woman could run, is all I can say. I bounced and swung on her hip till she was cut and bruised and bleeding all down her leg and we ended up in one of the great pipes leading off the reservoir itself. The water was icy cold and something happened to me that hadn't ever happened before. I fell asleep. I don't remember dreaming, or doing any of the things that you humans do, but when I awoke, there were four other bricks lined up beside me. All with the same type of face, all exactly the same size. The only difference so far as I could make out was that we each had a separate number. Same serial, but different numerals. Cookie was looking at me peculiarly. She had a grin on her face. I think, if I am not mistaken, that that was the first and only time I ever saw her smile.

'Congratulations,' she said. 'You've reproduced.' She ran her long brown fingers over numbers twenty to twenty-three in quiet amusement and I knew without her having to tell me what she was thinking. We were going to make a wall. First we had to find all the other bricks that were lying around and then dunk them in water – there was a hard glitter in her eyes when she thought this. I think it reminded her of an advert she'd seen somewhere of someone dipping biscuits in a cup of coffee. Then we were going to divert the water all over again. Only this time behind an impregnable fortress.

By the time she'd swum out of the reservoir again and found her way back to the vaults, there were another twenty of us and I still couldn't remember a damn thing about it. Naturally, she had to leave them behind, but she took me with her. It was night-time again when we got back home, and her grandmother was worried sick.

It took another year before she could gather enough people around her to try again. This time there were some men in the group, swaggering and loud with a let's-go-at-'em attitude. Cookie's grandmother was uneasy, and she forbade her to mention anything about me to any of them. Personally, I wouldn't have worked for them anyway had I suspected them of selfish motives, but she wasn't to know that at the time. There was only one young man amongst them with whom I felt I had some kind of accord. He came from a rich background but he was on our side. You could tell. Ned his name was, since you're so keen on labels. Are you people still obsessed with sexuality? Yes? Well then, you'd probably be interested to know that he was gay, too. Not that that's particularly relevant in my view, but you people seem to have a need to categorize each other. Why you can't be content with numbers I'll never know.

Anyway, the upshot of all this was that our small group planned a takeover of the deep water reservoir, followed by the building of a brick wall to keep out the State Police. This was all very well, but we were in the twenty-third year of the First Great Drought and so security had been tightened up drastically. Especially after Cookie's gang's last assault on the place. So, when it came to the hows and wherefores of this new operation, neither Cookie nor any of the other women got a look-in. It was suddenly decided, without any warning, by all the men – Ned included – to build a brick wall around the State Police Department first, and *then* to launch an attack on the water authorities after that. But only Cookie knew where to get more bricks, of course, and Ned was delegated to try and prise this piece of information out of her.

By this time the people were literally dying in their thousands on the streets. Every day dust-carts swept the precincts and the shop doorways clear of their thin huddled bodies, and every day the hygiene 'copter sprayed the area with a pungent smelling disinfectant that caused babies to develop rashes and adults to retch violently. Pretty soon people were dying from the after-effects of spraying as well as from dehydration. Then the authorities realized that it was also beginning to affect the upper classes, so they stopped it, and employed teams of convicts to hose the streets down instead.

It was a hard decision to make, but in the final analysis, Cookie felt she had no option. She had to tell them.

'Listen to me, Ned.' She was holding him firmly by the shoulders and looking earnestly into his eyes. 'It goes no further than our group. Once it gets out how we do it, we'll be finished. All of us.'

Outside, the temperature was already climbing into the low hundreds and it was still only ten o'clock. I remember that because Ned said he'd have to wait until dark before he went out to tell the others.

'Fancy a beer?' he joked. Neither of them ever had any money despite her job and his rich parents, but he was fond of her and he liked to try and cheer her up. She might have smiled for the second time in her life then. I might have seen her laugh even, were it not for the fact that the State Police kicked the door down at that moment and arrested them both for involvement in anti-state activities. They rounded up the whole gang during the course of that day and took them all down to the State Police Department in New London. They took me, too. Exhibit A. No longer number nineteen, I was a witness to one of the most infamous trials of the century. Except that it never did reach the papers. The government didn't want people knowing how to reproduce bricks out of water and using them to defend themselves. So it was all hushed up. New Fleet Street were told it was a bomb trial and they believed it. Britain may have been shrinking in the swelling waters of the North Sea and dying under the glaring heat of a naked sun, but at least it had been saved from terrorism.

How did they find out? I don't know. But I've always felt that it had something to do with the wrist-watch that Ned's parents had given him when they discovered he was gay. I suppose you could say that his sexuality was relevant in this particular instance. He was a subversive, you see. In their eyes, I mean.

Cookie? No. I never heard anything more about her. She might still be in that high security place for all I know. Funny how a government that condemns its own people to death by thirst and starvation should feel so squeamish about capital punishment. I've never understood that. Especially when your police are instructed to kill as well. Have you ever thought about that?

What? Who knows I can think? No one as far as I know. She never told them. Not even Ned. And if she did, they probably wouldn't have believed her anyway. Yes. I am shatter-proof. It's all true, I tell you. Everything I've said. If you don't believe me, try finding your own brick. There's plenty of us about. They can't have found every single one. You only have to look.

Don't leave! What are you doing? Who are all those women standing over by the door with hatchets in their belts? Mrs

Price will – her too? My God, why didn't you tell me? I can't feel everything from in here you know. Well, what are you standing about waiting for? Get this thing open. Let's see a bit of action for once. It's been too quiet here for far too long.

A Day Out

Janet Whalen

Mother vanished one day, seemingly into thin air. She didn't say where she was going. There was no indication she was going anywhere at all, she just went. I didn't see her go I just noticed she wasn't there. I noticed there was no tea in the pot and the kettle was cold. There was no breakfast on the table. I cursed her under my breath, and then out loud. I shouted my displeasure as loudly as I could and made my own tea, burning my hand on steam from the kettle.

I made enough for one only in case she decided to show up in the middle, in case it was a trick to get me to make the tea. Thinking better of this, I made enough for two – just in case. I can't stay mad for long. I'm so forgiving. She didn't turn up anyway.

I walked round the house. I was looking for notes. She must have left one, it didn't make sense not to. It just didn't make sense. No note. I looked in the pantry and tried to gauge which coat she'd taken. I sniffed the air trying to tell if she'd taken the unusual step of putting perfume on. I checked the post to ascertain what time she'd left, it was still on the mat. I felt Sherlock Holmes would have been impressed with my efforts. But there were no clues anywhere. Nothing to work on.

I stood in the hall and scratched my head, puzzled. Suddenly I stopped feeling puzzled and felt sorry for myself. How could she do this to me? Didn't she love me? No, she didn't love me. I'd become angry now. I tried to kick the cat which was still avoiding me from last time – it sidled hurriedly past.

When she finally deigned to arrive home it was gone tea-time.

'Put the kettle on, will you?' she said as she struggled in at the kitchen door with two large shopping bags. I'd spent the day sulking and was consequently tired out, but she didn't seem to notice. I was playing it cool and put the kettle on without a word. I'm not asking her, I thought.

She put down the heavy shopping bags and grinned

mysteriously at me. I smiled casually back.

'You'll never believe what happened to me today,' she said, with what I thought was an air of triumph. I waited for her to go on while I stirred the tea, watching the tea leaves chasing each other for the second time that day.

'You know those massive flying-saucer things you see on TV, on *The Twilight Zone?*' I was non-committal. 'Well, one landed in our garden today.' She paused to watch my reaction. My hand froze only for a split second as I handed her the tea. I gave the air a quick sniff for any trace of alcohol. There wasn't one. I decided to take a sarcastic line.

'Oh aliens, that's funny, they usually only call on Tuesdays and Wednesdays don't they? Today's Friday.'

'I knew you wouldn't believe it,' she said, taking off her shoes and drinking some tea. 'I wouldn't have believed it myself if I hadn't seen it with my own eyes. A blinding white light came out of the sky early this morning as I was putting out the milk bottles. I hadn't even had my cup of tea yet.'

This part of the story I could confirm.

'It was sort of glowing silver metal, it filled the whole lawn and one foot was in your dad's geraniums. I just stared at it.'

'I'll bet,' I said cynically from the sink. Maybe she's been working too hard lately I thought, and shot a sideways look over to see if she looked drawn and haggard. In fact she looked extremely healthy – I was the one feeling drawn and haggard.

'Anyway, they invited me up for a spin in the saucer – they don't call it a saucer but their language is too sophisticated for us. They speak really good English too, with a bit of a Scottish lilt, they say they picked it up by intercepting Glaswegian airwaves.'

'Look Mum,' I broke in, 'are you feeling all right, not tired or anything?'

'Never felt better,' she said, 'guess where we went?'

'Err, the Moon?' I decided to play along until help arrived. I didn't want her turning nasty on me – not with her sitting so close to the knife drawer.

'Oh no, I fancied the Moon myself, in fact the alien said you haven't lived 'til you've seen the sun rise on the mountains of the Copernicus Crater, though they do say the Moon has no atmosphere. I asked if that was where we were going but the alien said "Negative, our ultimate destination, Mrs Williams, is Alpha Centuri", I didn't feel in a position to argue, but I did point out that Asda closes at eight tonight and I had the shopping to get. Apparently they do have supermarkets on Alpha Centuri but you know what he's like about his food. They said we'd be back in time so off we went. Lucky I had my best slippers on. Aliens look just like us you know, except green...'

'Green?' I said.

'Yes, like the curtains in the back bedroom, sort of "bottle" I suppose you'd call it. Anyway it was ever so friendly. It said it liked Earth but couldn't understand why our buildings seemed to sprawl so much with no real pattern to them, and it hadn't realized there were so many Earthlings called McDonald. Anyway I had a guided tour of the Milky Way, that's our galaxy if you didn't know. Beautiful it was, all them stars.' She lit a cigarette and stared into space. 'Huge whole worlds just hanging there like pictures in an art gallery. Silent and peaceful like.'

'So anyway you got to Alpha Centuri,' I prompted, quite curious now. How could I have been living with this woman all my life and not realized how vivid her imagination was.

'Oh yes, well we landed – no parking problems, it was incredible, how can I describe it?... Remember that day trip to Bolougne we had last year? Well it was a bit like that.'

'Alpha Centuri is like a day trip to Bolougne?' I said in disbelief.

'I said "a bit", in the sense that things were similar but different. You knew you were somewhere else – there was a change, a different kind of atmosphere. It was warm and bright, there was a sense of peaceful harmony. The grass and trees were all exotic colours and everything seemed to bask in some kind of sunlight. Everyone seemed so happy and friendly, of course I couldn't understand them but they all waved and smiled. Not like here. Apparently it's always like that, I didn't want to leave. Anyway they dropped me off at Asda in time. We were back quick because we went through a time warp so I got all the shopping done.'

There was silence in the kitchen while we were both deep in thought. She sighed suddenly and then said, 'I did think about you and your dad while I was there. I felt a bit guilty, nipping off into outer space like that without a word, leaving you to cope while I'm gallivanting about the galaxy. But then funnily enough, I couldn't think of one single reason why I shouldn't. I thought, do I really need permission from my family to leave the Earth's surface if I want to? All these years I've looked after other people, now it's my turn.'

I shifted uneasily. I hadn't thought of it quite like that before.

'Funny how you take these things for granted,' I muttered.

'Exactly,' she agreed, 'so get your own tea, will you, I'm off.' With that she was gone again only this time I could hear her moving around upstairs.

For a moment the sheer lunacy of her story fell into the background as I realised what a lazy selfish little sod I'd been. I felt like a ball and chain. I felt as if I had somehow thoughtlessly stolen my mother's life from her. I resolved to change, and as soon as mum had finished any psychiatric treatment or whatever she might need, things would be different.

I was basking in the warm glow of self-righteousness and benevolence as she came downstairs with the best suitcase.

'Err, off out then?' I asked.

'Yes I'm off for good actually, forward any post would you, oh and look after the cat.'

A melodic electronic humming noise filled the air and the kitchen brimmed with this white light I'd heard so much about. A gleaming metallic saucer-like capsule daintily touched down on the lawn, with one foot carefully positioned in the geraniums.

'See you then,' and with a cheery wave of the hand she'd gone. When I looked, the thing in the garden had gone too.

I went out and peered very hard at the grass. I moved my hand about in the air and tried to stay calm.

'Did you see that?' I said to the man next door who was busy de-slugging his lettuces.

'What?' he said gruffly, 'did I see what?'

'Nothing,' I said and slunk back into the house.

'Where's your mother?' said Dad when he came in from work.

'Alpha Centuri,' I said glumly.

'What, again?' he said and turned on the television.

'What shall we do?' I demanded. 'She isn't coming back.'

'You'll just have to go down the chip shop,' he said.

Reflections in the Afternoon

Alrene Hughes

When you leave somewhere behind and return many years later it is not the things that have changed that surprise you, but the things that have remained the same. This country was once my home. There's where I went to school. There's my grandmother's house and the woods where I played from dawn to dusk on warm summer days. I drive along this road a stranger who knows every twist and turn.

My son is becoming impatient. I have promised him a beach and sandcastles. His father is not with us so I must play football too. I tell him we are nearly there. Round the next bend I know a canopy of trees will arc the road like a gothic window and as we emerge from its cathedral-like coolness into the warm sun the bay will stand deserted and idle before us. All the bays along this coastline are the same, each eating into the land producing an effect like scallop-edging on a tablecloth. I park the car and we carry the trappings of summer, bucket, spade, ball, rug, on to the sand.

I always remember places with ease but people and events get blurred around the edges in my mind. Maybe that was why I got such a shock on seeing the wooded headland of the bay. No, shock is too sudden a word; this memory crept through my eyes and washed over my brain like the tide creeps through a deserted mollusc shell lying on a beach. The sort of memory we edge further back from over the years because we know it could wear us down if we let it wash over us day after day.

It was on that headland that Michael asked me to marry him. I was eighteen and the last thing I wanted was to be tied down. We had been fishing that evening. Mackerel were fat and plentiful in the bay. Rumour had it they fed on the dirt the dredger boats churned up as they plied their way up and down the coast keeping a channel open for the big ships. We didn't care. The fleshy meat was delicious roasted over an open fire, and generations had feasted on them with no ill effects. I knew if I were to climb the headland now I could turn over with my toe the burnt out ashes of recent fires.

Michael hadn't understood when I explained about my dream. A fantasy he had called it. I was determined to leave this country to see things, do things, and somehow, though I couldn't have put it into words, I wanted to be changed, to become something I would never be if I stayed. What was wrong with this place Michael had demanded. Was it not a good place and what was wrong with being yourself?

I helped my son make sandcastles; the damp sand made sharp, steep sides to the moat and towers, but the tide was coming in and I knew that soon the castles would be smoothed and moulded into a uniform roundness so that only we, who had made them, would know what they once had been.

He wanted to play football now on the grassy area beyond the path. Not yet I told him, first we'll walk round the coast into the next bay, it wasn't far. He was a good child, dutifully held my hand, ran and skipped alongside me chattering all the time. But in the warm afternoon his voice mingled with the sound of the birds, insects and the lapping sea and I heard nothing but my own thoughts.

Twenty years had passed since Michael had proposed. I left him, my family, my country, soon afterwards. At first things went well, I had a sense of being in control, of shaping my life but in the end I succumbed. Succumbed to the inevitability of what life has in store for women like me. The tide of life ebbed and flowed wearing me down, smoothing out ambition until in the end only I remembered what the dream had been.

The walk to the next bay took longer than I remembered and I could feel the excitement mounting inside me. I was sure I knew what it looked like, but what if it had changed? Would there be a sweep of white sand and a lone white house standing full square to the wind on the far headland? It was Michael's father's house. Michael's now. He had wanted us to live there if we married. It's a good house he said, we could make it how you want it. I told him if I lived there I would paint it apricot. He'd been appalled. The house had always been white; it was a sort of landmark known to all the seafarers along the coast. Well, it hadn't mattered in the end.

The child was tiring at my side. Almost there, almost...there it was spread out below me, the same, the very same. Twenty years had been like one breath to it. As it breathed in I stood here a tall willowy girl with long auburn hair astride a bike, one foot on the ground to balance while scanning the beach for a slim dark-haired boy. It breathed out and I was a woman with a child. And if I had the chance to speak to that girl who was here a breath ago what would I tell her about dreams and reality?

There wasn't a coast path around this bay; here land and sea had no mediator but merged in an uneasy compromise of dunes and twitch-grass. We climbed down on to the sand. There was more shingle here than in the other bay and the current had cast up a flotsam of wood, cans, seaweed and shells in a broad sweep across the sand. A woman and a small boy were making their way across the beach towards us. They walked slowly with their heads down scanning the shingle and debris. The boy frequently picked up things then discarded them. The woman was more selective, occasionally bending down to examine something closely.

I had not thought to speak to her but my son ran off to play with the boy and when I sat on a rock she came to join me. She looked familiar, about my age. Her eyes were weary and there were lines etched in an arc shape on either side of her mouth but whether she had acquired them through laughter or anguish it was impossible to tell. What I did know was that she reminded me of myself. She expressed some surprise at meeting strangers on the beach and I explained that I had known this place as a girl, but had left some years ago. With the sort of reckless candour only enjoyed between strangers who know for certain they will never meet again, she began telling me that as a girl she had dreamt of leaving, seeing and experiencing new places, getting away from the unrelenting sameness of her life. I wanted to tell her it would make no difference, we stay the same and the same fate awaits us wherever we go. Instead I asked her whether she lived nearby. She pointed to the white house standing square on the headland and said she lived there with her husband and son. I admired the house and she told me that it had stood there for three generations always painted white as a sort of landmark to those who sailed this stretch of water. But, she confessed, she had always wanted to paint it another colour. Then she laughed, embarrassed, and said that she had dreamt once that it was apricot. Why not, I said.

The boys ran to us flushed and laughing. She stood up and so did I. Two women facing one another each with a child by her side. The same. Reality and fantasy. And like two mirrors facing one another the same image was reflected in each over and over, one behind the other. Generations of women with children looking at reality in their own faces and finding that their fantasies were doing the same.

I took the child's hand and made my way back across the deserted beach to my husband waiting for us in our white house which stood square on the headland and as I did so the setting sun bathed it in a warm apricot glow.

Sea Witch

Cathy Bolton

It is a steep scramble down the broken cliff to the cove. Gulls glide in the warm salt breeze, smooth as gondolas on a Venetian street tide. They make flight look easy. If my own wings were not clipped with cynicism I should drift in their wake. My skin is sticky with sweat. Reaching the sand I undress, tucking my clothes safely into the rocks.

Standing on the shore the waves sniff and lick my feet like an eager puppy. Cool turquoise sprinkled with sunlight stretches before me. Tempting me.

'The sea is charmed in these parts. It's not safe for bathing. There's many a tourist been drowned off this coast.'

The landlord's warning prises open an anxious gulf in my mind. Casting my eyes over my thin weak body I wonder if he would give the same advice to a man.

Slowly I inch my way in. Lungs clench as the coldness pockets my breath. Exhilarated, I push against the current. Twist in its tight embrace, measuring its strength. Trusting its magnanimity I let it cradle me. Float with my eyes shuttered against the glittering sun.

Something cold and papery washes over me. Cautiously, my fingers enquire, expecting seaweed. Brittle leaves scrunch and snap in my fist. Standing, they swirl about my waist. Thousands of silver leaves. Thin as foil, sharp as blades. They slice into my skin as I wade through rustling banks to the sand. I scoop them up in my arms but they float away like feathers. The beach now is a dazzling bed of jewels. A rich mosaic of rubies, emeralds, sapphires. My feet scorch and blister as I pick my way across these burning gems.

Cadgewid put some more peat on the fire. A week's supply gone in one night. It was worth it to watch the stranger's face reflect in the orange glow, as she lay dreaming on the sack-covered bales. She had the beauty of another world. Soft features and fine, smooth hands. A body unused to hard labour.

A gentle tapping distracted Cadgewid's meditation. She opened the door to Kynan's daughter. Her face pale and drawn like the waning moon gleamed out of her dark hood. Her words broke like foam on granite, Cadgewid's spirit unperturbed.

'Oh Cadgewid, they think you poisoned Ruan's son. You've got to get away. They're going to do something terrible. It's the holy man. He's told them you've got evil powers. That we need to rid you of this evil before it consumes us all.'

Cadgewid beckoned Kynan's daughter in towards the fire. She smiled apologetically at the bewildered stranger, surfacing from sleep.

I am running across the rocks. Craggy limestone rocks, rutted with pools. Waves explode about me. White flames leap up between cracks, snapping at my legs. My feet seem to know where they are going. They find safe landings. Do not rest to let me contemplate my next step. The rocks are patterned with swirls of colour, like oil on water. I should like to examine them more closely but I am travelling too fast. Adrenalin surges through my body giving me new strength. My muscles sing to be alive. I have never been this close to happiness.

The sky was still heavy with coal when the men led Cadgewid down to the shore. Rough hands gripped her wrists unnecessarily. She did not resist their demands. Walked as dignified as she could, shackled by those burly men, down the muddy slipway. There were more villagers waiting on the beach, huddled together around blazing torches. Their faces spoke of more fear than her own.

'This is for your own good,' the holy man explained, as another roped her body to a rock. 'The sea shall cleanse you of the evil that possesses you, and your soul shall be saved.'

The women dug their feet into the sand for warmth. Avoided Cadgewid's questioning gaze. Many of them had made secret visits to her cottage on the moor. Confided in her desires and fears they could not entrust to their husbands or each other. Gratefully they had received her knowledge and healing remedies. If Cadgewid were guilty of communing with evil then they too were tainted with that crime. Guilt it was that froze their hearts and tongues. Only Kynan's daughter made her protest public. Her screams ripped mercilessly into the darkness. Her lack of conformity did not go unnoticed. A dutiful child, the holy man thought, but she would have to be made an example of.

The rocks now are almost vertical and I have to traverse this endless wall. My fingers and toes caress it. Pick out small pockets to tuck into. I am exhausted but I cannot will my body to rest. Beneath the sea slaps against the cliff, regular as a heartbeat. The rock no longer feels cold and hard but warm and fleshy. My hands clasp other hands. They lift and carry me onwards.

Cadgewid gave herself quietly to the sea. The tide bit free her bindings. Dragged her out like more dead wood, then returned her to the shore filled with new life. Her salt-bleached brow rooted in the shale. Conurbations of limpets anchored in the fertile bone. Small crabs crawled through sockets that last held jellied images of hungry waves.

A tungsten sky hung over a restless sea. Gulls screeched in the dull gloom. With long sticks the fishermen rocked Cadgewid's skull against the stone. They still feared her magic. They had been foolish to listen to the holy man. Alive, her deeds had caused them little harm. Some had been robbed of unborn sons. Others resented the cunning she had taught their wives. Mostly they had benefited from her powers.

Her spirit absorbed by the sea was more powerful than ever and bent on vengeance. The coast was littered with chunks of gnarled wood and tangled nets. More than half the boats and many lives had been tossed against the cliffs in the months that followed the drownings.

Cadgewid gave herself quietly to the sea but Kynan's daughter did not. She struggled hysterically against her executioners. The holy man would not let them put an end to her suffering. She must go to her redemption fully conscious. The women and children had to go back up to the village to protect themselves from the sight of evil leaving her body. They could not sleep for the sound of her distress echoed on the wind. At dawn Cadgewid came to comfort her. Embracing her in watery arms, stilled her pain.

There is no moon to point a path through the maze of gorse and heather. It snags my skin, and makes my legs weep with blood. I have been running for hours. Close to the edge for the sound of the sea is reassuring. It is the only sound to be heard. I do not know where I am running to but my body craves motion. It will not stop.

I see a small building ahead. It shades a faint glow of light. I pray my eyes do not deceive me. Someone is walking towards me. A woman. Cloaked in magenta. Her face is warm. She takes my arm. I think she must bear my weight for my legs feel so light. She takes me into the stone room. It is infused with the smell of strange herbs. She sits me down in front of the fire.

'You have had a long journey,' she says, passing me a bowl of hot sweet liquid. She feeds me freshly smoked fish. It is as if she has been expecting me.

She examines my nakedness with kindness.

'Your poor body. Let me tend it.'

She washes the blood and sweat from my skin then rubs pink and green ointments into my aching bones. I feel like a helpless child. Thirsty as a sponge, I soak up her tenderness. She wraps me in linen and tells me I should sleep a while.

I am woken by rasping whispers. The woman strokes the hands of a girl who is trying to push words past tears. I cannot make out her strange accent only that she speaks of great danger. The woman turns her smile to me. I think I must blush. I feel a little ashamed for I know that I have held this woman in my dreams. That I have taken more than comfort from her pale lips. My skin still smarts from the passion of her kisses.

'Do not fear. They cannot harm me. No one can harm me,' she is telling the girl.

I believe her.

The Thirteenth Blessing

Alison Guinane

To start with, there were too many godmothers at that christening. Made it look worse that I wasn't chosen – the event having been long awaited.

Only Miriam could have found a name like Rose-Briar – full of sweetness and fragrance, fairytale charm. Well, being sweet and passive had helped her to the top, and I suppose she felt it her duty to do the same for her daughter. No sooner had the midwife declared it a girl than she was soothing her husband's patent disappointment (he had of course hoped for a boy) by murmuring plans for marriage. A neighbouring stockbroker, father of a sickly son, had friends in all the right places – and beneath the gold bonds in his inside pocket beat a patriotic heart. Here was Rose-Briar's shining hope for the future, puling in his nursery.

And there was Albert's well-known chronic superstition – his passion for even numbers, absolutes like dozen or score. He would disintegrate into a state of psychotic terror at the mere thought of thirteen. As a single woman living alone, not in my first youth, I inspired him with a healthy apprehension, as squirrels watch lizards climb trees.

I was the unfinished story, the beetle in the blackberry pie, and I made people feel uneasy at social gatherings of a ritualistic nature. My only offspring died in infancy and I never married the father. He didn't even know – a ringed fence put around my past and a small house in the mountains till it was over. I was bundled off with my bulge so it wouldn't spoil Miriam's prospects. And I was never forgiven.

There is a dark place still somewhere inside me, with a closed door, and for a long time the effort of avoiding it sapped my strength.

But there was power residual in my knowledge. There remained the fear of what I might say. Refusing to be personal slave to some pin-striped portmanteau, I chose deviance: to associate with those who lurk in the drizzle on dark corners, and who screech incoherence at passers-by. Too odd ever to be taken seriously.

I looked odd, too – my hair a mass of knotted darkness, skin as brown as a fox's earth. (A by-blow of my mother's some would say on one of her numerous pseudo-diplomatic excursions.) I was forty-five – an age when women look about, take stock. Also an age when labels are attached firmly. Labels are misleading. They tell the brand-name or the price, and nothing else.

Much was being made of the only birth in the family for a decade: gilt-edged invitations, cake as tall as a spire. Presents were arriving most of the time – so many they would have to be given away. The godmothers would be traditional and give theirs at the christening party – which meant they had to spend weeks thinking up the unusual.

At first I decided I wouldn't go and returned the invitation. Then the day before the christening it occurred to me that I was going to be there. She was my niece. And I wanted to give her something.

I wasn't noticed at first in the crowd, sliding between hats and salmon patties. I wore my black velvet jacket (to give me mystique) and hovered in a corner, feeding the corgi.

Miriam had a chiffon creation on her head, covered in pink and lilac flowers, and a white patent shoulder-bag swung on a flimsy strap over her shoulder. When Albert had finished bumbling on and the tables had rocked at his hundred-year-old jokes (inherited with the Rolls Royce and regalia) Miriam put on her public speaking voice and announced the presentation. She smiled around graciously beneath her spotted lilac half-veil.

One by one the twelve godmothers (deep bosoms generously roped in pearls) minced up to bestow their offerings. The men stood about perched in corners awkwardly, like so many stick insects clinging to walls. The baby was the only one there with a purchase on the future, and she was asleep.

There was nothing very extraordinary: gold bracelets too heavy for the child to wear, fluffy animals four times her size, a christening bowl.

Eventually I marched up at the end of the queue and placed my book on the satin counterpane.

A shocked pause was followed by a general intake of breath. Indignant whispers caused the baby to wake and gaze at me in amazement. I fell in love with her then – her eyes wide and green as apples. Miriam was clutching the edge of the table, her knuckles as white as the linen cloth, slightly unsteady on her gold spiked heels.

I made my speech, 'She will spin the texture of freedom and clothe herself in a web of grace and power. When she is sixteen let her find me and I will teach her all she needs to know.'

Gradually I became a recluse, living alone in my flat at the back of the house next door, talking to the birds which I fed from my window or Sycorax, my cat. I kept company with the shadows, made things, wrote things, was not afraid of hardship. Sometimes in summer there'd be barbecues and the smell of charcoal would coat all the leaves in the garden. A quiet numbness settled in, the passive defiance of nature's last defence.

While Sycorax slept by the fire, conjuring bats, I digested my wrongs. Couldn't they see that I was trying to add and not take away? I wanted her to be strong as well as beautiful, creative as well as marketable, with faith in her destiny and the will to control it. Not the sort who lies helplessly until someone arrives *en scene*. Then the usual collision with reality...

It was hard when she didn't even know me. That was very hard. I watched from my window, saw her grow. She talked to herself while dismantling roses, trying the petals on her fingernails or sat between roots of trees, reading aloud till dusk.

It wasn't time yet. That would come, soon enough. So I chose concealment in my upstairs room, rotating yarns and old remedies. Waiting for spells to wind up.

I don't think I was mad (though some accounts have said so). It's just that I grew out of people very early on, as I grew out of flimsy dresses. I had disturbed the time-honoured complacency of the occasion in order to celebrate the truth in advance.

The sixteenth year was a golden one. Not being very academic, young Rose-Briar couldn't wait to leave school and Miriam

was full of her public appearances, her clothes, her prospects.
(Particularly her marriage prospects.) The stockbroker had
made his second million and been elevated to the peerage, but
couldn't be persuaded to leave his car-phone long enough to
take his seat. (His son wore horn-rimmed glasses and was
something at the Foreign Office.) There was a thicket of
admirers to complicate matters, but it seemed generally
understood that eventually he would be the one to carry off
Rose-Briar in his white Mercedes.

The photographs showed her serious and thoughtful. No
push-button simper to oblige the crowd. There was loneliness
in her face and she was too thin. I felt sorry for her, with her
protuberant bones and skeletal frame so prominent beneath
the expensive drapes... She was probably anorexic. Such a
common complaint for girls her age...

At Christmas it was her birthday and all the lights came on.
A big celebration would be in order, and there were rumours
of an engagement. I could imagine only too clearly the
enormous enjoyment Miriam would be getting out of all the
fuss, her indulgence in neurotic planning... For instance, how
to obtain the obligatory flowers (so few in season – and one
wouldn't wish to be common by having only those) and then
make sure they didn't wilt in the central heating?

It was cold. The coldest winter we'd known. Yet I felt a
sense of secret distension, like the ache of waiting to give
birth. I took a fresh bundle of tangled wool, slightly sticky with
its film of grease, and skewered it firmly on the distaff.

Sycorax slowly uncurled from the woven rug and arched her
black back lazily. Tail-tall, she padded punctiliously to the
solar door. She knew what time it was.

Snow had fallen and the trees shivered under swansdown
cloaks. Distant lights blurred between branches and muffled
music leaked under doors.

A party of young people, streamers looping party clothes,
bobbed along the path. One of them sang, loudly and tunelessly,
but then forgot the words and subsided into giggles.

It was dusk and shadows were thickening.

There she was.

She lagged behind and followed the cat to the solar, ruining
the velvet dress which trailed behind her up the fire-escape

stairs. She paused a moment, while snow dissolved around her, then twitched with irritation as the door banged.

The light from the fire caught a shock of spiky hair, conker-bright, with glints of green and orange like a wood-sprite's. A black butterfly edged with marcasite was clipped above one ear. The eyes (I remembered them well) too wide apart. The mouth too generous, for fashion, but resilience lodged in the turn of her chin.

She came and stayed of her own accord – though the rhetoric of myth-makers would one day claim differently.

Sap froze in the roots of the forest as the viscosity of life solidified. Fish were trapped under ice in the brook and the birds were silenced. A few last apples, crisp with frost, hung like baubles on the medlar trees, forgotten. The holly bushes bristled round our little fortress, with great red berries dropping on the snow, sealing-wax on vellum.

To primroses and lavender add peppermint and sage, half a pint of rosewater, a handful of rue, the secret root of valerian... Taken at sunset infused with herb-of-grace, induces dreams free from sorrow...

She would gaze at the flames and tell stories to the fire, till they came.

That, at least, was traditional.

The Burden

Thea Parker

Freda sank thankfully into the first seat on the bus, exhausted and annoyed at her own stupidity for thinking you can carry the same amount of shopping at sixty-two as you can at twenty-two. She wedged the plastic carrier-bag down in between her feet and was grateful that she had caught the number nineteen instead of her usual bus. This was what they called the 'local runabout' and would take her miles out of her way, calling at every corner of every estate and giving her a chance of a good sit down without having to feel guilty about it.

She gazed out of the grimy window, seeing parts of town she hadn't been to for years – not since Dad and she had gone to live in the Yorkshire Dales with Gran, after Mum had died. That would be almost a half-century ago now. Most buildings had been replaced by modern shops and tall storey offices, but every now and then, she caught sight of something familiar, and memories came flooding back into her mind as she recognised more and more places where she had been so happy and where she had grown up. Excitement mounted as the little single-decker rumbled on, slowly because of the innumerable stops to set down and pick up. She decided then and there that she would get off soon and have a walk down Granby Avenue to see her old home. It would be interesting to see it again after all this time. Forgetting about the weight of her shopping she requested the driver to stop at the end of Granby Avenue, and without as much as a trace of a limp or flagging footsteps, Freda set off to look for number ten.

The houses were still pretty much the same. Most looked very dilapidated and shoddy. A few had been recently painted, and some had even had extensions built onto them, but in the main they were 'tatty' and ill-kempt. Number ten was here now, on Freda's right. The iron gate was still missing – nobody had bothered to replace it since the council took them all away during the war to help munitions. What amazed her was the fact that the pink, green and grey mosaic triangles of concrete which Mum had saved up so hard to have laid, were still there today, undamaged, and looking just the same as when they had left. The little garden too, to the left, was exactly the proportions it had been, even down to the little circular patch of soil in the centre with a few large stones forming the rockery. The windows, too, were obviously the original ones, with the stained-glass transom window in the front door. That had been painted a horrible shade of yellow. How Mum would have hated it. The knocker looked as though it hadn't been cleaned for years. Much to Freda's surprise she found herself feeling a little superior and brave enough to lift the knocker. Goodness only knew what she would say when someone came, if indeed there was anyone at home at all at three o'clock on a sunny afternoon in June. She could pretend she was looking for someone and make up some fictitious name. She just wanted to have a closer peep into her old world – who knew, she may never have a chance to come again in her life time. Her plastic bag grew heavier the longer she waited. Her right arm was beginning to get unbearably painful and her shoulder felt as if it would come away from its socket. She knocked again. Oh, please come, please come, she thought, I really can't stay here much longer. Then Freda heard footsteps coming down the hall. They never seemed to arrive at the door though. She knocked again, louder this time.

'Please come – I'm getting tired and feeling a bit dizzy. I can't stand the weight. It's my right arm. Open the door, please.' The footsteps grew nearer and heavier and louder. 'Open the door, please – I can't stand holding on any longer – help me...'

Mum's blue overall with the pink flowers moved up and down to the rhythmic heaving of her ample chest as she cradled Freda's head down to it.

'Stop your crying now, child, you're safe. I'm glad you came at last – I wondered how long it would be. You should have come to say goodbye such a long time ago. Why did you make your life such a misery?'

Freda sat up and dried her eyes. She looked in wonderment at her dear mother's face, as young and pretty as she remembered it.

'I thought you knew, Mum. I thought everyone who had died knew what was going on in our heads. Dad told me you had gone to heaven and that I must be brave and not cry. I was a brick, he told everyone. And that was what I turned out to be – a brick – with as much feeling and soul. They all thought I was brave, not crying or carrying on that I had lost you, but they didn't know I couldn't cry. I would have given the world to be able to have done. I had no feelings at all. Everything that you had planned for me to do – all went away. I left all my studies, gave away my books, cancelled the scholarship, and went off with the first chap who asked me to marry him. We had two children, both boys. One of them looks exactly like you, Mum. Now they are grown and both left home with wives of their own. If only I could have mourned you, Mum. If only Dad had come and put his arms round me and let me cry, instead of expecting me to be so grown-up I could have been normal and fulfilled all my ambitions. Mum, help me...'

The three women who stood chatting at the end of Granby Avenue turned round to watch the ambulance drive away.

One spoke, 'Poor old soul, I don't know who she was – didn't come from round here. Expect that big load she was carrying was too much for her.'

The Curse of Brandverd

Cath Staincliffe

It's the sort of story you'd love to tell your grandchildren, I often do. I was on the Valetta when she made that trip, it was the high point of my career. It's been taken up as a modern myth now, a catchphrase; 'like a future on Brandverd' they say, meaning a thing that cannot be for obscure or hidden reasons.

I'd been a patroller-gatherer for a good few years, mainly on the old abandoned bypass system. There'd been a wealth of colonies out there, centuries ago. All long gone. We copied any interesting cultural artefacts, checked on general environmental stability and entered a patrol survey of each planet or station visited. It was a fairly steady methodical line of work. Quiet too. Occasional travellers, starcombers and enthusiasts were the only people we met.

But enough of the bypass. Brandverd was another kettle of fish altogether. For a start it was at the other end of the spiral, there'd not been any contact in all the centuries since the Exodus and it was as mysterious to us as Uranus had been to Terran spacers. There'd always been speculation about whether human life had developed there. Radio signals had never been answered, scans had sent general impressions of a green planet with adequate atmosphere, but no one knew whether colonists had ever even reached Brandverd.

It's listed on the sacred rolls from Terra: 'To Brandverd – the Traveller and two hundred souls'. One of the thousands of passenger launches during the Exodus when the planet had become uninhabitable. While other pioneers had remained in contact and cultures had evolved, some leading to our current societies, from the far end of the spiral there had been only silence. Myths had grown up over the years. Brandverd was peopled by mutants, they lived underground, cannibalism was rife. A world of demons, to frighten children with.

The planners decided to back a search and recovery. It was the chance of a lifetime. Few of us get the opportunity to travel so far. When the voyage was announced it was as if I'd heard my name called. There were four of us selected, none of us had crewed together before. My fellow gatherers were all women, not unusual really but I was pleased. I always seem to get good luck on an all-women ship. Call it superstition.

The youngest of our crew was Yasmin. Linguist and physicist. She was small like me but dark skinned, dark haired. Her broad knowledge complemented my specialization in the Terran vernacular and social structures. I knew the swear words, the slang, while Yasmin was *au fait* with the grammar and the classics.

Carla, our geologist and archaeologist, was a big woman; tall, broad, larger than life and full of it. A mane of wiry, ginger hair framed her pale, freckled face and grey eyes.

Our fourth was Gerry, bio-ecologist. An older woman, she wore her long, grey hair pulled back from her face and had the blue eyes and pink complexion of those whose ancestors came from North Terra Eurobloc. Gerry was a healer and meditator. I hoped to improve my meditation skills with her help.

Not a day too soon came lift-off. I said a sad goodbye to my little girl who was in cover-care. I sometimes took her with me on short trips but being cooped up on a ship wasn't much fun for kids and a long haul was definitely too much. I'd arranged for friends to see her, for a holiday with my mother and some time together when I got back. I promised to send her tapes whenever I got the chance. I felt a lurch of anxiety about her as we prepared for take off. My way of dealing with separation. We'd be okay.

The haul out was long but uneventful. I spent my days preparing for the quest, reading up on potential cultural patterns, social structures, sexual mores, slangs, langs and dialects. As a group we soon gelled. Carla and I became particularly close. Attraction of opposites perhaps. When I could tear myself away from all the things I wanted to get on with, I got on with her.

As we neared our destination the ship took on more and more the feel of a laboratory. Each of us busied ourselves preparing films, tapes and containers in order to document, measure, label and categorize our booty. Carla ran a sweepstake on what we might find on Brandverd. I thought they'd probably have made it to the tenth century but being this far out would not have survived the cold of the Dark Age. Carla reckoned the Traveller never reached its destination. Space travel wasn't exactly a commoner's garden in those days. Yasmin's bet was on a successful landing but a failed colony, some natural disaster. Gerry refused to speculate. Giving us one of her more enigmatic grins she simply stated that she'd dreamt we would meet somebody and nobody. None of us believed we'd encounter any living people but I couldn't help having the occasional secret fantasy...

We locked into orbit overnight. None of us slept well as we were eager now to be on world. The scout we sent out reported back reasonable climate; hot and humid atmosphere, breathable, if a little high in oxygen. Lower gravity than home but enough to keep our feet on the ground. No radio or sonar waves, no large noisy centres. We identified a plain suitable for landing, glacial in origin and giving us plenty of room for manoeuvre. We all hugged each other for good luck. I closed my eyes and clenched my teeth as we descended. The landing was as smooth as a baby's bum.

My first glimpse left me with an impression of overpowering greenery. Growth on a massive scale, unlike anything I'd ever seen. Towering trees festooned with creepers, a thickly woven carpet of lush shrubs and bushes. The landscape was designed to match. In the distance great sand-coloured cliffs and escarpments rose up, streaked with waterfalls plunging down to dark gorges. The scene was breathtaking, a little overfacing. As if things had run riot, grown out of natural proportions. We rechecked our readings and, assured of the safety of the air, put on working overalls for alighting.

Outside the place smelt salty, pungent and earthy. It was warm. A sunny day. The sky was blue like home but much deeper reflecting the tone of the greenery below. We stayed close to ship all morning, preparing the tourers for gathering and finding our balance. We had to adjust to the gravity, the sensation of things being lighter; the way it feels when you lift a new-born baby after having lugged a toddler around. We let off the scans. They went zigzagging towards the cliffs. As yet we had no inkling whether anyone else had been here before us. Carla was busy gathering samples of rock, earth and sand for testing. Gerry gathered a handful of snails with patterned shells. She told us it was likely there'd be some form of bird life with the abundance of bird foods; seeds, weeds and snails, though none of us saw or heard anything.

We stopped for lunch and called in the scans. They'd been flying about all morning, plotting and replotting maps of the area. Yasmin went in to feed their tapes into the scan bank and left them to compute. Carla suggested that we eat alfresco so we all brought out patties, beer and bread and set up a little picnic. The beer and heat lent a party atmosphere to the occasion. There we were, a little group of women, hundreds of thousands of miles from home, clinking glasses, making jokes, nerves of anticipation fuelling our laughter. We were heady with the adventure of being there. I was dying to see what the scans would show. I hoped it would back up my hunch to head up beyond the sandy crags. It made sense to go for the highest point unless the atlaspic showed evidence of settlement elsewhere. I mean, there's one thing beings like us do, wherever we roam. One of us goes off and climbs a mountain and finds a few stones to mark that visit. We'd also be able to see more from a high vantage point though the dense forest might hide small settlements. I drained my glass and interrupted the others.

'Come on, I can't wait any longer, let's see what we've got...' I felt giddy as we went in to see the simulations. The scans had covered several square miles that morning. I held my breath as Gerry pushed the display, Yasmin was hopping from foot to foot with excitement.

'Hell's teeth,' exclaimed Carla, 'civilization.' My stomach turned over. We were looking at a small village, a handful of single-storey buildings, stone built, on a small plateau above the cliffs.

'They made it,' whispered Yasmin, 'they really made it.'

'But are they still here?' I asked, my blood chilling with the thought. Would they communicate with us? Attack us in fear? We'd be gods or devils. Not of their world. Aliens.

My eyes searched for clues about the likelihood of life. The scale of the map wasn't large enough to show small objects. I couldn't see a well or water source near the dwellings. The picture was grainy and blurred but I noted there were no obvious paths or walkways. The scans do take into account surface make-up and a well-worn path through the village would have shown up. If anyone lived here there'd be paths. Unless they'd learnt to fly. I was pretty certain we'd find no one. No one alive. I breathed again.

We recapped on standard procedures for initiating contact, how to minimise the likelihood of conflict or violence. We were in the tourers, ready to leave, within the hour. Carla and I took the guideship while Gerry and Yasmin followed in the slow, clumsy one we called the donkey. They were heavy but reliable, hovering ten feet above all obstacles. As little children we'd called them flying carpets and built pretend ones in the sand.

'Well,' sighed Carla, 'looks like I lost the sweepstake, maybe we'll find a welcoming committee, mutated homo exodus.'

'No chance,' I said, 'no paths, no people.'

'Maybe they use tunnels,' she quipped and threw me a wink. I flung my head back and laughed at the idea.

Within half an hour we'd clambered up the west side of the cliffs and overland to the village. We hovered a while before landing just outside, on an area of heathland. We walked towards the settlement. In real sight everything was shabbier than in the simulation. There were five rectangular buildings, one set a little apart was larger than the others. It would probably have been for communal use; to store or prepare food, to meet in, worship or dance in. The other buildings would have been accomodation. The doors and windows had gone long since, we were looking at the shells. If times had been particularly hard they'd each have housed a family so the whole community would only have been twenty or so. There'd probably have been similar set-ups elsewhere on the planet unless this had been a splinter group of some sort, victims of illness isolated from the rest or separatists for religious or political reasons. Surely a luxury on such a far frontier. As we reached the clearing in the centre of the five I was convinced that we were alone. Total silence, the lack of domestic noise. The absence of clutter, tools, buckets, ropes. The litter of human life was missing.

We observed protocol even though it was obvious everyone was out of town. Yasmin and I stood back to back in the centre of the clearing while Carla and Gerry set off to check the buildings. We saw them disappear into the doorway of the nearest one. Creepers and weeds had taken hold and fringed the sandy stones of the buildings.

'Why such a small place,' mused Yasmin, 'outcasts perhaps...'

Carla's shriek made us both jump. We raced to the doorway and peered in. My heart banged in my chest.

'It's okay,' Gerry was quick to reassure us, 'we're all right.'

'Bit of a shock,' said Carla, 'look.' She moved aside and I could make out, in the far corner of the room, lying on the floor, a skeleton.

'You scared the life out of me,' I complained.

'Blame her,' said Carla nodding towards the corner.

'It's a woman?' asked Yasmin.

'Yes,' confirmed Gerry taking a closer look, 'no obvious sign of injury.'

'How come she's just lying there?' Yasmin frowned. 'How come no one...' she broke off.

'Maybe there was no one else around.' I shivered. There was an awful sense of loneliness here. Imagine being left, deserted, isolated. It's our first and most fundamental fear.

'The only girl in the world,' chimed Carla. I winced. Sometimes her frivolity was misplaced. I felt a little in awe at our first discovery and disturbed at the mystery it presented. I wasn't in the mood for jokes. Nor were the others. Gerry and I exchanged glances, giving Carla the benefit of the doubt – after all she'd had the biggest shock. I hid my irritation.

'People always bury their dead if possible,' said Yasmin, 'something must have happened, something that ended up with her being alone.'

'Let's just check there aren't any more,' I said. We looked round the other buildings and returned to the first.

'Nothing,' reported Carla, 'well, a few artefacts but no people.'

It was then that Gerry spotted the parcel. At the side of the woman's head on a low slab of rock, smothered with dust, was a small metallic folder. Inside were what became known as the Brandverd Diaries. Every gatherer's dream. We knew they were the key to the story of this place.

Returning to the ship with the folder, Carla and I discussed our find.

'What do you think killed them off?' she asked.

'If they were killed off,' I replied.

'Well it doesn't look like they thrived, does it?'

'Could be a virus.' Measles obliterated Delta Pluto and our training station had once seen its students decimated by bubo bubo.

'I think there's something weird going on,' Carla announced melodramatically.

'What do you mean?'

'It all looked too neat, too orderly. As if she knew.'

'Maybe she did. If it was an epidemic she'd have seen the others...'

'Life's not like that though,' Carla interrupted, 'it's messy, it doesn't run smoothly. S'pose she was dying, knew she was last, how come she didn't collapse in a heap...'

'C'mon Carla. If you feel ill you lie down. Once you're down you don't want to get up again. Maybe she'd had enough. Suicide. Or just lay down and died. People do you know.'

'It must have been awful for her.' Carla sounded as though it was the first time she'd projected her imagination into the situation.

'Being the last you mean?'

'Yeah,' she looked away from me and out of the window.

We drove on in mutual silence. Below the abundant undergrowth was tinged with late afternoon sunshine. Greenery shone and glistened. I barely noticed. What would it have been like to be the last? Would she have been beseiged by panic? Fear stricken? Or was it something she came to terms with? In my own fantasies I saw myself nobly choosing suicide. A prepared and ritual death, a letting go.

Back at the Valetta we ate a simple meal and listed our initial tasks. Yasmin and I would concentrate on opening and logging the metal folder. Script on the outside suggested it contained writing. The other two would return to the area and undertake a general geological, archaeological and ecological survey of the place. I said my goodnights and had a shower. It was disappointingly cold and didn't relax me at all. However I fell asleep as soon as I hit my bunk.

I woke halfway through the night. Terrified. I sat upright and turned on my sidelight. In the nightmare I'd been free floating and struggling for breath. Grasping for a cable just out of reach, cycling my legs in a futile effort to get closer to it. To get away from the thing behind me that was holding a hand over my nose and mouth. My mouth full of broken teeth which fell and scattered as I screamed...

I breathed in slowly and regularly until I'd reduced my pulse rate. I resisted the urge to get up and wake someone. It was only a dream. It had been a tense day. If it still troubled me in the morning I could analyse it with Gerry. I drifted back to fitful sleep. I think we were all haunted that night. Carla and Yasmin looked tired and preoccupied at breakfast. Gerry didn't join us at all. Nobody talked much and I think we were all relieved to go about our business, absorb ourselves in the routines of work.

The next few days were a blur of intense activity. While Yasmin and I painstakingly separated, snapped and recorded the flimsy parchment inside the folder the others spent most of their time over at the settlement. They found graves nearby, half a dozen skeletons of older people with nothing to indicate death from unnatural causes. Dental evidence proved these to be original pioneers from the Traveller. Disease or virus wouldn't necessarily show up on skeletal remains. We remained uncertain as to what had caused the demise of the colony. Initial geological surveys didn't indicate any major fire, flood, earthquake or drought. The struggles that had sculpted the mountains and carved out the gullies and waterfalls had taken place aeons before the Traveller had landed on Brandverd. To Gerry's disappointment there were no birds. The eco-system consisted of rich plant life, a number of small insects, flies and aphids, beetles and molluscs and bacteria. The snail was in effect king of the jungle. It was a quiet place as a consequence.

Neither Yasmin nor I could sightread post-Terran fluently but we got a sense of the work in documenting it. It seemed to be a journal or history of sorts. We lost all the beginning and chunks of the last third, which crumbled as it was handled. Entries were in many hands, perhaps the job of scribe was rotated. We were terribly impatient to get the copying done and start the actual work of translation. Over the first few days some obvious patterns emerged; an entry of betrothals each spring, a big shindig in the winter. I felt overall there was little material. I expected more from the diary of a colony, more comings and goings. It all seemed a bit thin. I hoped once we knew what all the words added up to we'd get a fuller picture of what happened to those people.

Gerry took the donkey out a few times but saw no other buildings. We let the scans off but all they relayed were more great forests, mountains, valleys and rivers. Any other old settlements on lower ground would quickly have been overgrown. After a week we still hadn't a clue as to why the pioneers had died. Dispirited we agreed to take an evening's R. & R. together. We made a luxurious meal, opened a couple of bottles of vino and spent a few pleasant hours getting gently stewed and talking. The evening ended with great hilarity as we imitated birdsong that we so missed from home. As I stood to go to bed I clapped my hands for attention.

'Gatherers...' I began.

'Go and get it!' they joked.

'Listen,' I held up my hand, 'silence please. A little respect. Tomorrow we begin translations.' I bowed with a flourish as they clapped and cheered. We were all tired of speculating. Our initial intrigue at the mystery had turned to frustration. Like a riddle that goes stale. We wanted to know. We all put a lot of hope into the writings.

'You wait,' teased Carla, 'they'll wind up being the shuttle timetable.' The others giggled.

'Knitting patterns,' Yasmin chipped in.

'Weather reports.' Gales of laughter.

Our first day translating confirmed that there had been some sort of spring festival when betrothals were made. The first entry I worked on described one. Luckily the language was pretty close to base and a lot of the popular references were familiar to me. The writings charted the story of the colonists but not on a daily or weekly basis. Entries appeared to be made whenever anything worthy of note happened. It seemed that the journal had been open to all, it was written in many styles. Some of the entries were highly personal, others less so.

'The party returned today. Abroad for more than a year. They have made precious maps. There is a great lake about a month's walk south of here. Some of our rivers run there. Tom thought it was the sea but there was no tide, no waves – just a vast saltlake.'

We lost the next few pages the next legible entry read: 'The corn's in, beans done well. May and Obi suggest new strains and extending crop rotation. There's no opposition but precious little interest either. No pleasure in this harvest for me.'

'Seems a bit apathetic,' I remarked.

'Maybe it was all very easy,' suggested Yasmin.

'Perhaps she hated farming,' I added. We carried on. The next few entries were fairly mundane arrangements for plot cultivation and the building of a storehut. Then we found a death notice.

'Rosa Levin died. Age thirty-three. Accidental death. Rosa drowned while swimming below the falls. We remember her with fondness and love. May she rest in peace.' Then we were back again to another list of spring weddings, formal and repetitious.

'There doesn't seem to be a lot here for a year,' said Yasmin.

'Well, we lost a few entries. I guess life was just very quiet,' I replied.

I couldn't get to sleep that night. The ship was as quiet as the planet. I'd been in my cabin earlier laying down tapes for my little girl. I got to wondering how it must have been for those women so long ago, having their babies on a strange and unfamiliar world... Of course! There hadn't been any babies. We hadn't translated any births – that was what was missing in the records. We'd found betrothals, a death but no one was having children. The colony hadn't been killed off, it had died out. Why?

The crew of the Traveller had been selected for their health and fertility, their willingness to go forth and multiply. What could have caused their sterility? Viral infection? Radiation? If they'd been radiated on Terra they wouldn't have passed the medicals. Perhaps some sort of sunburst en route? I debated whether to wake Yasmin. In the end I let her sleep. It could wait till daybreak. I dozed. I woke from a dream in which I was giving birth to lots and lots of tiny skeletons who bowed and then walked off up the high sand hills. By first light I'd decided to suggest to Yasmin that we should select paragraphs with key words in to translate rather than progress chronologically.

She needed no persuasion. We searched through for passages that included the words for child, children, infertile, baby and barren. We found several laments from women about their inability to reproduce. For some it had acquired religious significance, the punishment of some vengeful god. Others poured their bitterness on the heads of the politicos who'd planned the Exodus. Most were just downright grief-stricken that there would be no pregnancies, no births, only great yawning emptiness.

'What are we doing here? We have come too far. It was never meant to be. We are the lost generation. No roots, no fruits.' There was no future for them, nothing worth investing in. Crops, cloth, shelter were useful only for the lifespan of the colonists. The young men and women had come all this way with dreams of a new world only to find themselves sterile, useless, trapped on a blighted world.

'I will never hear a baby cry,' one woman wrote, 'nor the sound of children's laughter. All the future holds is getting old, dying, death.'

'We will have no sons, daughters, nephews, sisters. No human relations. Dry as dust.'

'In the midst of such abundance we are barren. We are barren and our hearts are broken.'

It was well past supper-time when we adjourned to the kitchen and shared a cold snack with Carla. We told her how much we'd divined and where our search was leading. The tests she and Gerry had carried out on the skeletons from the graves corresponded to our information. Most had died of old age with no sign of unusual disease or injury. None of the women bore the wider pelvic bones associated with childbearing. Geological and ecological surveys hadn't revealed anything untoward.

'Maybe back then there was something in the water, some toxin that acted as a contraceptive,' I suggested.

'Not likely,' Carla shook her head.

'Perhaps it was the journey,' said Yasmin, 'the conditions were pretty primitive then.'

'It's most likely to rest with the women,' said Carla. 'It's difficult to suppress sperm production, it's a continuous process. The ovum are all there from birth, if they all got damaged...or maybe something disrupted ovulation.'

'What? What would cause a healthy group of women to all

become barren?' I asked.

'Some massive hormonal change,' said Yasmin.

'Like premature menopause you mean?'

'I don't see that,' said Carla, 'I can't think of anything that would result in mass sterility.'

We'd worked a ten-day stretch and needed a break. We arranged a day out, exploring Brandverd on foot. I got up early. The thick mists were turning mother-of-pearl colours in the sunrise. We set off into the dense forest, so unfamiliar to us. Back home we were used to flat sandscapes and marsh, to wide skies, the constant cries of terns, gulls and waders. We had some tree cover but nothing on this scale. Our progress was slow due to the heavy undergrowth. Tall, fleshy, pink flowers filled the air with a sweet, heady scent. It was uncannily quiet. The soft buzz of a fly, the burble of a stream the only sounds. We ate our picnic by one of the myriad streams, bathed in its clear water and forgot for a few precious hours the strains of work. Sunset came early and the nights were dark here so we made sure to get back to the ship in good time.

The following morning we began work with rekindled energy. We relocated our search around new key words: Brandverd, disaster, accident, sickness, poison, in the hope of uncovering the cause of the infertility. For several days we translated flat out. A tale emerged of the breakdown and fragmentation of the colony. The burden of grief was so great it corroded the foundations of the society. Theft and assault are mentioned, virtually unheard of in so small a group. Several writers curse Brandverd which they regard as a poisonous paradise, a Garden of Eden concealing Hell. The community became split and divided.

'We have chosen to part, scatter ourselves across this place. I will go with the other single women. We will have more peace in smaller groups. We have had enough of strife.'

As they grew older they were all aware that one of them would eventually be the last, the end of humanity. That burden had fallen to the woman we found. She had buried her compatriots, written the final entries. Waited. It got to feel like we'd never know the reason why.

I met Gerry in the kitchen one break.

'You were right, you know,' I said.

'What about?'

'Meeting someone and no one.' She smiled, offered me a cracker.

'Thanks,' I took it. 'No ideas what went wrong, no hunches?'

'No,' she replied, 'I've dwelt on it at length, I can't see it clearly. Have you established whether they were ovulating?'

'I don't know. There's no suggestion of miscarriages, they refer to themselves as barren. That suggests they weren't.'

'It would have taken them a while to realize something was wrong after the trauma of the Exodus and the journey.'

'Yes,' I agreed. We were all familiar with the menstrual disturbances caused by space flight. Off-world there's no day and night, the sun's always shining. On the Valetta, as on other ships, we create an artificial day and night using shutters. But the combined effects of disorientation, stress and physical pressure causes many of us to miss a period or skip ovulation. Pregnant women rarely run the risk, the chance of miscarriage is too high. Some spacers take pills to keep regular. I prefer to let my body sort itself out. I don't like to suppress upsets. It's unlikely any provision was made for those early travellers. For some time any disruption of their cycles would have been put down to the voyage.

'But sooner or later they should have recovered, settled down.'

'No more clues?' Carla came in, her thick hair coated with dust from her latest sampling.

'You're sure it rests with the women?' I asked her.

'Absolutely,' she was emphatic, 'to sterilise a hundred fit young men you'd practically have to boil their balls.'

'No mention of that,' I laughed and returned to work.

'Marie died last night, she was the light of my life. I will miss her so.'

'Died Juan Margoles, age sixty-six. Heart attack.'

By tea-time I was feeling depressed. The journal had become little more than an obituary column as people aged. I went to my cabin and tried to meditate. I couldn't concentrate. There was a knock at the door. Carla's head appeared.

'Fancy a walk?'

'In this dark? We'd never find our way. It's black as jet out there. Gives me the creeps.'

'Funny,' she sat on the end of my bunk, 'people complain about Axon 'cos the nights are so bright with two moons and here...hell's teeth!' she screeched and leapt up.

'Carla, what's wrong?' I thought she was in pain.

'It's obvious, it's been here all along...get the others...'

'They're in the lounge.'

'Come on,' I clattered down the ladder after her.

As she began to speak I realized the answer had been right under our noses. There'd even been a clue to it in one of those first diary entries. The saltlake had been a sea, but different from the seas we know. It had no tides.

You see on Brandverd there is one essential prerequisite for human life absent. There is no moon. No moon to wax and wane, to beat the rhythms of life, to pull the tides and turn the cycle. No moon to orchestrate the dance of time, to illuminate the night, to make us mad. No moon, no month, no monthlies.

Nowadays few people read the diaries though we all know the story. It was the final entry that stuck in my mind, like a tune I couldn't shift. It suggests that they probably guessed the cause of their plight even though the connection between the moon and fertility was regarded as mere superstition back then. It was the last word from the woman we found, we think it is a poem.

> 'I am grief
> Frozen in space
> Star stunned
> O can you hear me
> Across the spiral.
> I am lost
> Drowning in the dark
> A shell of emptiness
> O can you hear me
> Along the Milky Way.
> I am done now
> All will be silent
> And I will join the stars
> I have had enough
> Crying for the moon.'

Froddo – The Perfect Man

Jane McNulty

She slammed her pencil down and reached for the glass. As she gulped the wine she rubbed at the throbbing pain in her temple, her eyes shut tight against the light from the desk lamp.

'You drink too much of that stuff,' he said.

'Mind your own business,' she snapped in return. He shrugged.

'Please yourself, but just don't spill any on me.' Preening. She thumped the button on the base of the lamp, flooding the room with darkness and, dangling the empty glass from two fingers, she staggered to bed, alone. The paper she had been working at glowed on the desk, pale in the street light from the bare window.

'Good morning.' The sarcasm was delicate, pointed. 'You look terrible.' The man sat easily on his chair, one ankle crossed over the other. She groaned and held her head in both hands.

'Oh, for God's sake, Froddo, give it a rest. I feel like death.'

'Here – draw me a coffee-pot: you need something to bring you back to the land of the living.' Froddo's joke. She drew an elegant coffee-pot.

'Two cups.' The man got up and stretched. 'I'll join you.' He moved across his white background, humming – very pleased with himself – and finally came back to his seat with two mugs of coffee, white for him, black for her.

'Thanks.' She sipped her drink: it was very good. He always made good coffee. He watched her, leaning forward in his chair, his elbows on his knees, feet wide apart, ready to pounce. Wait for it.

'You can't keep doing this to yourself.' So that was to be the ploy today: fatherly, tender. It was a difficult one for her to fight, it put her off guard.

'Froddo, look: I enjoy the odd glass of wine. What's so wrong with that?' He shook his head. Damn him, damn his understanding smile!

'Odd glass? Melanie, you drank two bottles of the stuff last night. And your work's suffering. Just look at my hands!' She looked. He was right – his hands were badly drawn, like two bunches of bananas. Stab of guilt to the stomach.

'Oh Froddo, I'm sorry.' She took the eraser and removed the clumsy hands, gently blowing the bits of rubber away.

'Ooh, I love it when you do that,' he sighed suggestively. She drew quickly and with skill, adding two strong, sensitive hands to the edges of his shirt-sleeves.

'Okay?'

He held his hands out in front of him, turning them over. He nodded.

'Fine. Just the way I like them. Now, you've repaired me, but what about you? What are we going to do to mend that broken heart of yours?'

What indeed. When Froddo had a problem (which he did occasionally have during the course of a particular story-line) Melanie could just draw in a solution or write in a clever one-liner, redraw the edges of his life and make things all right. But when Simon walked out of her life a month before there was no way she could do the same for herself. No magic eraser would take away the pain that swamped her, there was no trick she could use to fill the empty space inside her. Just the wine, and that made her feel worse the next day. She picked at her nails.

'I don't know why I keep getting hurt like this. I'm not a little kid, for Christ's sake, I'm a mature woman with a nice flat, a successful career, no money worries. I should be on top of the world, having fun, living. Instead what do I do? Spend my evenings moping around here because I've fallen in love with some beautiful man who has turned out to be a bastard, a liar or a dirty old man. Or married. Men I know are going to hurt me; but still I do nothing to protect myself. It keeps on happening. You know, Froddo, I'm a danger to myself. I ought to be kept in until I learn sense.' Bitter. It made her feel so tired. Froddo folded his arms and looked directly at her.

'Maybe that's what we should do.'

She put down her empty cup and asked him to explain.

'Well, you have the answer right here. Froddo, the perfect man, or rather, you could make me so. You simply have to take your pencil and create your ideal man. Dark or blond, friendly or mysterious, whatever shape and size you prefer – it would be your choice. Then you write the story-line, only of course, you put yourself in there, too. Draw yourself – right in here with me, and we'll take it from there. What do you think?' Froddo leaned back in his chair, rocking slightly on the two back legs with his hands clasped behind his head. So simple! Melanie and her perfect man living in the crisp background of her sketch-pad with no lines out of place, nothing blurred or smudged, just as she wanted. Perfection.

'Let me think it over, okay?'

He agreed, still smiling, so sure.

It was raining outside, great stair-rods of cold, driving rain from a navy blue sky. On her way home from the hairdresser's, the MG had broken down on double yellow lines and she was drenched as she walked to the flat by a taxi speeding through a flooded pot-hole. By the time she reached home her hair was flattened to her head, her make-up ran in sad trickles down her chin and the french bread hung limp over the side of her shopping bag. She threw her wet things in a heap on the kitchen floor and poured herself a drink. A large one.

'That won't help, you know.' Froddo, the smug sod, shaking his head.

Melanie stood under the shower for a long time letting the hot water sting her cold skin, turn it red and blotchy. She soaped and shampooed herself until she felt squeaky clean: the road grit washed away down the plug-hole. Wrapping herself in a towel, she poured another drink and sat by the fire with a small sketching block.

'What are you doing? I can't see from here,' Froddo called from the desk-top.

'Doodling,' she replied. 'Just working something out.'

It was growing dark when Melanie returned to her chair and switched on the desk lamp. She held up the sketches for Froddo's approval.

'Not bad,' he murmured. 'Not bad at all.'

She took her pencils and began to draw, working fast but with definite strokes. First Froddo, tall and lean with dark wavy hair and a firm jaw.

'Moustache?'

'Hmm, yeah, but no beard.'

'Right.'

Then furniture. Clean lines, lots of light from high windows, a hi-fi.

'Don't forget the bed,' Froddo leered wickedly.

'Men!' Melanie pretended to be exasperated, but she was secretly excited at the thought.

'Now for you.' Froddo sat on the edge of the bed she had just drawn, following Froddo's suggestions, circular with mirrors above and all around. She paused, just for a moment, then began to draw. The figure was basically Melanie but enhanced and superimposed with an ideal she had: legs longer and slimmer, hips trimmer, belly more flat, breasts...?

'Froddo?'

'Give me the pencil.' He held out his hand while Melanie drew him a pencil. 'Like this.' He drew breasts on the figure, larger and pointed, uptilted.

'Impossible,' laughed Melanie.

'Nothing's impossible here, my girl. You can have what you want. Anything you want. And I want them like this.'

He added volume to the hair, fullness to the lips, a smoulder to the eyes. Melanie as a sex-goddess – she felt herself blushing.

'That's not me,' she said, flattered.

Froddo turned his back to her and used the pencil on himself, erasing a little, adding a little, all going on out of sight, but she could guess what he was doing.

'Just giving nature a little help – a minor embellishment.' Froddo gave her an innocent grin. Melanie giggled, turning a deeper shade of crimson.

'Now make yourself comfortable,' he patted the mattress, 'and Froddo will make everything better.'

Saturday night, Sunday morning, the days had no beginnings, no ends unless they drew them for themselves. They played jazz on the hi-fi – Froddo's choice, Melanie made coffee, Froddo sat in bed with the papers. She came over to where he was with a tray of warm croissants and fresh coffee, sliding in beside him under the duvet, wrapping her body around his. He turned a page.

'You know, Melanie, I really enjoy reading in bed,' he mumbled through a mouthful of croissant. Flakes stuck in his moustache and fell into his chest hair. 'You should have drawn them for me before.'

While Melanie covered his body in butterfly kisses, Froddo munched his food, slurped his coffee, and carried on reading his paper. Finally she gave up and picked up the colour supplement. The cartoon pages were missing, ripped out: Froddo said he didn't like her reading the cartoons in case it reminded her of her former life.

'Former life?'

He smiled indulgently at her.

'You don't regret coming here, do you?' Little boy, hurt.

'Of course not. It's perfect here. I just wondered how they would fill in my page, that's all. I mean, what would the *Sunday Herald* be without "Froddo" and his smart outlook on life?'

He didn't say anything, just pulled her towards him, kissing her hard. They spent the rest of the day making love; in the bed, in the shower, on the kitchen table.

'Like having a delicious meal,' Froddo licked his lips.

'Unhygienic,' Melanie wrinkled her nose in mock disgust.

Later they lolled by the fire – sketched in by Melanie as the winter light faded – and Melanie traced shadows on Froddo's bare skin. She was falling, falling with that familiar hot chill, that sharp softness, that sweet sourness, and she felt warm, and sleepy, and safe.

When she awoke the fire had gone flat, not out, because it was still there where she had drawn it, but it gave off no heat and no light. It was a cartoon fire in a cartoon room. Froddo was nowhere to be seen. She got up and wrapped her bathrobe around herself, it was hard and stiff like paper, as was the carpet, the sofa, the bed. She was alone in the white room. Even through the high windows, the world was stark, two-dimensional, and Froddo was gone. Melanie beat her fists around the edges of the paper and shouted in a thin voice.

'Melanie? Something wrong?' Froddo's voice. Unmistakeable.

'Froddo, where are you? I can't see you.' Desperate.

His voice came from outside the boundaries of the paper.

'It's all right, honey. I'm over here by the fire. I'm just putting the finishing touches to an idea I've had. Be right with you.'

Froddo had stepped out of the cartoon world and into the

world of full colour, the land of the living. His face, the one she had drawn for him, appeared above her, tanned, breathing and alive, and his hands so beautifully drawn to be warm and skillful held up a sketching pad for her to see.

'What do you think?'

Melanie, wild, pacing, looked up at the story-board. 'Melanie, Sex Slave.'

Froddo was proud of his work.

'Sent it to the *Herald* last week. Under your name of course. They liked it, Mel, they used it yesterday. Got a contract for a whole series. Not bad, eh? Better than that bloody wimp Froddo, anyway, with his smug, homespun wit.'

Melanie tried to speak, splutter her rage, demand he return to the page where she had created him, but his words covered hers out of sight.

'Bring in some real money, this one. Maybe film rights?' he moved around the flat, her flat, his body easy, confident. 'We'll have to make some changes, though, get some more light in here, a decent hi-fi.' He laughed.

'Oh come on, Mel, it's not so bad when you get used to it.' He was removing the cartoon pencils from the story-board where Melanie stood. He took his pencil and drew instead a bottle and a glass.

'Drink up, there's a good girl, Froddo'll draw you a new playmate.'

`Till Death Us Do Part

Sheila Parry

9th November, 2050.

This is the last time I shall write in my journal. Tomorrow is the Great Day. I'm finding it hard to concentrate but I know I won't be able to sleep tonight.

It's very quiet, sitting here alone on the fiftieth floor. From my window it looks so easy to step out among the stars or walk on the moon. Soon I may be doing just that.

After the frantic weeks and months of preparation everything is ready. All leading up to tomorrow – the day everyone assumes will be the most important in my life.

Meanwhile, my mind goes on checking lists like a manic computer. The food is organized, my daughter Zena saw to that. A wonderful spread of all my favourite foods complete with an enormous white iced cake in the old style. She called me earlier on the video-phone, looking unfussed and elegant as usual. She seemed concerned about me.

'Don't forget to take that special pill tonight,' she said, sounding like the highly-trained doctor which she is. 'You need a good sleep – it's going to be an exciting day tomorrow.' I promised I would but after she'd switched off I put them in the garbage chute. I prefer to stay awake – endings and beginnings demand a clear head.

The usual contingent of friends and relatives have been invited. They'll all be there, waiting in the church for me to arrive. Just think, it's taken me fifty-five years to make the centre stage and tomorrow that's where I'll be. Strange how churches have been kept going just for these occasions. No one goes to services any more. Not much point when no one believes in God any more, only in Man – and Woman of course.

Back to my lists. Flowers, for me and for the church. Zena arranged for these as well. I haven't seen the arrangements in the church, she wants them to be a surprise but my own white lilies are keeping fresh in the bath. I'm worried about the lilies.

Their beauty and purity won't show my ageing skin to advantage but Zena insisted. It's always easier to agree when she does.

I had my way over the music though. No modern electronic/computer discords for me.

'It's my day,' I said, 'and it's going to be my kind of music.' So it's back in time to 'The Wedding March'. Zena doesn't approve but that's what I shall have as I walk down the aisle.

I can just see the dress gleaming in the shadows of my room. Full length and silver, plain but beautiful. The most beautiful dress I've ever owned and what a waste – to wear it now, at my age, and for such a short time.

I'm beginning to feel sleepy now but I want to stay awake tonight. I'm afraid of the dreams which may come if I let go. In spite of the tablets I've been given over the past few months, I feel confused and apprehensive. Everyone has tried to reassure me and they all say it's a natural reaction – just nerves.

'Everything will be fine,' insists my son Dak. I hope he's right.

Dak's a computer researcher and he's organized everything for tomorrow. I could never have coped alone with all the form-filling and interviews with officials. It's not an easy matter to arrange – not at my age anyhow. Dak tells me that permission is a privilege but in his position he has influence with all the right people. Less advantaged citizens have no such elaborate ceremony to look forward to. I realize I'm fortunate to have a son like Dak.

'You don't need to worry about anything, Mother,' he assured me when the date was fixed. 'Just be there at the church, looking your best, that's all we ask you to do.'

The day is already beginning. I can see the first faint light of dawn creeping into the sky. It's my birthday, I'm fifty-five today. Not until this evening to be precise but that won't make any difference. By then I shan't be worrying about such details.

Thinking of my birth reminds me of my mother. She was eighty and very frail and she'd been ill for a long time. She suffered a great deal before she died – I mean, before she found Peace. At least old people don't have to go through that now. Anyway, there aren't any old people any more. It's better that way, I suppose. Easier on the relatives and costs the community much less than trying to keep all those old bodies alive.

I wonder sometimes, though. I remember my grandmother. I loved to be with her when I was small. She was so comfortable and kind and she had time for me. No one else did. I should like to have been a grandmother. Stop it – that's not allowed. Sentiment is destructive and is not encouraged. I had to forget that dream when Zena and Dak were awarded special promotions and privileges for deciding not to have children. I know I should be proud. I understand about the dangers of over-population. People said I was a good mother, I'd trained them to be right-thinking citizens. I only felt sad, for them and me. I'm not good at all really. That's why I'm afraid of tomorrow. It's a relief to admit it at last but there's no one I can tell. No one who would understand. After all, I agreed – didn't I? It was my idea – wasn't it?

I'll keep my mind on preparations for tomorrow – I mean today. I can already hear sounds of movement in my glass tower. Other people are starting their day too.

Soon I must have a shower and put on my silver dress. Zena will come to pin up my faded hair and cover it with flowers. Then Dak will arrive to escort me to the church. I mustn't let them down. No looking back, no fears, no memories. I want them to remember me today with pride. I'll smile for the photographer, knowing the instant pictures will look out from golden frames fondly displayed by my two brilliant children.

Somewhere a bell is ringing. I must stop writing and prepare myself to meet the waiting bridegroom. I must get used to calling him by his new name, the old one was so ugly and frightening. I must rehearse my final response, 'I take thee, Peace...'

Between the Lines

Sue Wright

'Lance, I love you but it's so painful,' sighed Sacha.

'Darling,' Lance held her with a passion so intense, so deep, they almost wept, 'darling, oh darling I know, but I beg you don't end it this way, not after all we've been through.'

'David Sheldon, room four please.'

It's time the tacky stories in women's magazines belonged to the real world instead of Mills and Boon land, thought Jenny as she turned the page on Sacha and Lance and why, she continued to muse, do they always have stupid names? Why can't Dorothy fall for Brian, or Kevin for Janet, or even Brian for Kevin?

Zzzzzzzzzzz, the drill was beginning to get on her nerves now. I wish the receptionist would close that door, in fact, she groaned to herself, why can't room number one be on the first floor instead of the ground floor, right next to the waiting-room.

'Dear Denise, My boyfriend is a lovely man, but no matter how hard he tries, he can't get rid of his BO.'

Give him the elbow dear Desperate of Plymouth, thought Jenny, now clearly showing signs of irritation at the constant terrifying noises from room one.

David Sheldon returned to the waiting-room rubbing his left cheek. Oh God, I hate it when they send you back in here to await the gradual disappearance of feeling in your mouth. Silence now from room one.

David Sheldon was sweating profusely – maybe he's Desperate of Plymouth's boyfriend, Jenny amused herself with thoughts of such a coincidence. Yes he looks like the sort who has BO, she decided! Don't be stupid, how does someone 'look like the sort' who has BO. In an effort to restrain a grin from appearing right across her face, Jenny flicked back a few pages to say hello once more to Sacha and Lance. She was pondering over how their affair had started, as someone had ripped out a 'twenty pence off Brillo Pads' coupon on the back of the opening paragraphs to 'Love Among the Stars', a steamy behind the scenes story of love and passion between two leading soap stars, during the long gruelling hours of filming on location in Acapulco. Oh yeah, thought Jenny, and how many episodes of Coronation Street are filmed on the shores of Acapulco Bay, eh? What baloney. Nevertheless she rejoined the saga...at least while her mind was in Acapulco her ears were half-closed to torture chamber number one!

'Henrique will not stand for it Lance,' cried Sacha. 'He's given me an ultimatum, I have to decide between him and you my darling, between the stability and respectability of a twelve-year marriage and five years of blissful meaningful romance with you.'

'It's more, much more than a romance Sacha, you know that. What about Gabriella? We both know that darling Gabriella is more than a product of a "romance", she's our daughter, born of love.'

'Lance don't,' pleaded Sacha. 'You know if Henrique ever finds out the truth about Gabriella he'll kill us both and himself too, that secret must go with us to the grave.'

'I won't live without you Sacha, I won't.'

A piercing cry shot through the air from room one. Oh no, thought Jenny, I can't bear this pressure. Jenny looked up from the hold of 'Love Among The Stars', David Sheldon was chatting nervously to the woman next to him. When he smiled at one of her comments, only one side of his face moved! Jenny smiled to herself at the sight.

Above their heads were the usual array of before and after gum disease posters. Yuck! I bet Lance has never had grotty gums, she reflected, in fact I can't imagine Lance sitting anxiously underneath mouths which look like they've been used as extras in 'Zombies Return From The Dead'.

'Pauline Wilson, room four please,' called the receptionist coldly. Pauline Wilson stood up, bent down for her bag and caught her tights on the chair leg.

'Damn,' she said with such feeling you'd think they were silk.

David Sheldon was quick to assist in unhooking the snag.

'Thank you,' said Pauline Wilson, meekly.

'You're welcome,' came the reply, 'it doesn't look that bad really.' Their eyes met only inches apart, as Pauline Wilson tugged at her skirt to try and cover the rapidly growing ladder. As she left the waiting-room, David Sheldon's eyes followed her every little move.

Aha, thought Jenny, love among the dentist's patients. Could this be the start of a tacky magazine love story? David Sheldon caught her stare, they both looked away, embarrassed, him towards the 'Ten easy steps to pearly white teeth' poster above the door, and her back to the tales from Acapulco. Maybe they met at the dentist's, she thought, now Sacha would be wearing silk stockings, that's for sure. How dare somebody deprive me of the birth of their beautiful affair for the sake of twenty pence off Brillo Pads.

'It's late Lance, I need some sleep...alone, I'll give you my decision in the morning.'

'Sacha, this is pure torture, we can face the scandal together, you, me and Gabriella. We have a future together, please darling, decide on us.'

'It's not that simple Lance,' sighed Sacha, *'Gabriella sees Henrique, and Henrique alone as her father, I couldn't change that, she adores him, and he her, I don't think I could be that selfish.'*

'Well leave Gabriella with Henrique and come to me alone, we'll get through.'

Sacha was hurt that Lance could be capable of making such a cold request.

'Lance leave me now, I'll sleep on it.' He leaned across the sofa to kiss her cheek but Sacha, unwilling to receive such affection from him, stood up. 'Bye Lance.'

'Next Thursday the 25th at 4.30p.m. Okay for you?'

'Oh, oh yes I think so,' came the muffled reply.

The door to the outside world opened and closed. David Sheldon looked up from assessing the contents of his wallet, towards the waiting-room door. I bet he's hoping that wasn't Pauline Wilson leaving, Jenny thought, don't worry though that was the poor victim from room number one. Pauline Wilson is still in the dentist's grip upstairs in room four, the very same dentist's grip which held you. Aah isn't that romantic! I hope David Sheldon and Pauline Wilson don't have to share the traumas of the Acapulco duo.

Lance was brought abruptly from his slumber by the deafening ring of the bedside phone. As he reached for it, his half-opened eyes read 3.36a.m. on the clock.

'Lance, it's me, Sacha.'

'Oh...Sacha,' came the drowsy reply, 'is everything okay?'

'Lance, I have to talk to you, I've made my decision, I'm on my way up.'

Prrrrrr, the phone went dead. Lance sat upright and turned on the lamp. His heart was racing as he pulled back the covers and stood up, wearily pushing his fingers through his tousled hair. He unlocked the door in anticipation of Sacha's visit, then walked over to the dresser, reached for the Scotch and poured some into a glass. The coolness of his drink came as a welcome relief to his parched mouth. As he rested the glass back into its original place there was a quiet, but firm, knock on the door.

'Come in Sacha,' he whispered. At the same time his heartbeat seemed to fill the room and the sweet taste of Scotch was now making him feel quite nauseous. The door opened slowly...

'Jenny Morris, room one please.'

The beads of perspiration were growing in number on Lance's forehead. 'Hello darling.'

'Hello Lance, I'm sorry to wake you, but I haven't slept at all. Lance I...'

'JENNY MORRIS, ROOM ONE PLEASE.'

'Damn and blast,' shrieked the voice in Jenny's head, which was lost in Acapulco. That very same voice which mocked such 'drivel' not twenty minutes ago. Jenny's heart raced faster than Lance's as she reluctantly dropped the magazine back onto the coffee table. David Sheldon was still awaiting the return of Pauline Wilson from room four. Don't get mixed up with her if she's married, Jenny wanted to advise him. As she left the waiting-room, she noticed Pauline Wilson walking back down the stairs. Oh good, at least they can be alone now, however briefly.

Jenny entered room one, her thoughts were with Sacha and Sacha alone. She began to wonder how she'd ever be able to get through the rest of the day, never mind the week, without hearing Sacha's decision. What if I'm not sent back with numbing mouth, into the waiting-room. Oh God, don't dare do that to me she inwardly shrieked at the dentist.

Don't be stupid now woman, remember that's Mills and

Boon land. It's simply garbage, mind-deadening, absolute unadulterated rubbish, nothing more, nothing less.

'Hello Miss Morris,' gleamed the torturer of room one. 'Do sit down.' As he altered the spotlight above her face he turned to the dental nurse and said, 'Well Sacha?' She gazed back at him.

'Of course, I'll stay, Lance...that's if you still want me...'

Medusa My Mother

Christine Wainwright

There is a courtyard. An inner space at the heart of a great white marble palace. Imperious in a purple robe stands the warrior prince. Huge dark and massy he stands, legs apart, arms across his mighty chest. Pale and submissive the young princess, little more than a child, waits before him. She studies her rose-painted toenails and the delicate golden sandals she wears upon small arched feet.

He cannot see her eyes, which some may say have a sly expression. In accordance with custom she waits to learn the nature of her marriage task, which she must perform before they can be married.

'Find the hag who is decimating my armies,' commands the prince. 'Hundreds of my warriors have disappeared, and we are sure this monstrous woman is involved. Find her and bring her to me, before the ninth full moon of the year.'

The girl lowers her chin slightly in acquiescence.

'There are rumours that she is sheltered by the mad women who keep watch outside the camp on the west side of the great plain,' the warrior prince declaims. 'My men are too afraid now to interfere with these women. What can soldiers do in the face of such magic, such strange powers? It is most unjust. However, you may be able to gain entry to their camp.'

Slowly, deliberately, he intones, 'Bring me her head. On the eve of our wedding, according to custom, the battle which has raged on these plains for years will cease. Friend and foe alike shall see that a great warrior chooses a woman worthy of the honour he bestows upon her. A woman fit to share his bed, bear his children, and be his helper.'

The girl, head still bowed, dips a knee and leaves. She will not be allowed to speak to him until they are married. How pompous he sounds she thinks, knowing she should not have such thoughts.

The scene changes. Woodsmoke spices the soft evening

silence around the camp on the great western plain. As the girl draws near, dressed now in plain dark robe, long cloak and stout sandals, the hazy silence is disturbed by the sound of women's voices. Around a fire the women talk, drink wine, and chant their women's songs.

There is a serenity about the place which puzzles the girl. She had expected to see strange mad creatures performing weird rituals or wandering around gabbling to themselves. These women are wary but friendly as they receive the girl into their midst. She feels no surprise however at this unquestioning acceptance of her presence. She is accustomed to privilege, and expects to get her own way, at least within the limits of her existence in the palace. Nor does she feel guilty. If it is necessary to take advantage of these trusting people to achieve her heart's desire, then that is what she will do. She is shown to a small shelter made of twisted branches and grasses, which will be hers for as long as she stays.

Soon she meets the woman she has been sent to kill. She befriends her and becomes her helper. Their daily work is to break up huge pieces of statuary which lie in a shallow pit at the far side of the encampment, away from the eyes of the patrolling soldiers. This woman, the girl's intended victim, is thin and very tall, with a sallow bony face and tawny, deep-lidded eyes. Her long wild hair, which seems to shimmer with many colours, has strands which shift and undulate, even when the woman is still. She lives in a hut beneath a giant pine tree, whose resinous juices scent the air sharply but pleasantly when the sun is hot. Sometimes white doves settle on the high branches, sharing their secrets with no one.

The woman tells the princess about her life. Soon the girl is aware of a bond growing between the two of them. The other women in the camp call her 'little sister'. The princess finds this strange, but wonderful. As was customary, she had been taken from her mother shortly after birth, and reared by kindly but indifferent nurses. She did see her mother and her sisters around the palace, but the women and the girls were discouraged from spending too much time together. She had never experienced the comfort and freedom of undemanding female company.

Eventually the girl asks the older woman why she hides with the mad women. Although she still refers to them as mad she often wonders now how they came to be called that. Her question is not answered directly and there is a brief smile at the girl's obvious embarrassment as she refers to the camp women as mad. The older woman does, however, tell the princess that being in the camp has given her time to think. And this in turn has changed her ways of looking at the world. She explains how she came to question the ways in which a woman's life is controlled by the laws of a society where all the power lay in the hands of a few men. She also tells the girl that she began to wonder why it was necessary to have the constant wars that raged over the land. She will not, at first, be drawn to say why she must hide.

As their relationship progresses the woman passes her wisdom on to the girl, although the girl does not realize this at the time. She is not yet aware that her own ways of thinking and looking at the world are changing. She still wishes only to perform the marriage task, return to her warrior prince in the city, and become his wife.

The princess discovers that the older woman's early life had been much like her own. High-born, she too had been reared to be an obedient wife and bearer of children. Her marriage task had been to steal certain magic crystals from the temple of a far away hill city in the north. These crystals were said to impart great wisdom upon their possessor, who was suddenly able to see things more clearly, and in much greater detail than before. Only the high-priest, the physician, and the ruler of the city had access to them.

After successfully stealing these magic crystals, the woman says, she had broken the taboo and looked through them. Immediately she had decided to keep them, at the same time resolving to marry if and when she chose. It had not occurred to anyone that a woman would dare to use the crystals. Such rebellion had never even been considered. Since that time, of course, she has been in hiding. Partly because of the unforgivable insult to her prospective husband, and partly because of the breaking of the taboo. But mostly, she says, because of what she has been doing since then.

Quite by accident she had discovered that the crystals possessed another power. Strolling one day along the camp perimeter, keeping to the trees to avoid the soldiers, she had just taken the crystals from her pocket. As she held them, she had been surprised by the sudden appearance of a small band of warriors. They had been sent to spy upon the women in the camp. As soon as she was seen the leader drew his sword and lunged towards her. He paused momentarily to swing the blade back and above his head. The others moved in closer. With no means of retreat she had stood her ground, still holding up the crystals and gazing defiantly at the men, who, unaccountably, halted and became quite still: all at the same moment. Not waiting to find out what had happened, she fled.

It was about this time also, the woman remarks, looking slyly at the girl, that her hair became quite unmanageable, so she stopped bothering with it, having other more urgent things to do.

Understanding that the girl is still committed to her previous life, she does not explain further. Nor will she show the precious crystals to the girl, but says she always keeps them in the pocket of her robe, in two small phials. She says she only uses them for peaceful purposes nowadays. Chipping away at the solid piece of stone before her, she smiles. And the girl, not understanding, smiles back.

Inevitably there came a time when, gazing one night at a sharp sickle moon, the young princess realizes that her time with the women must end. Soon she will have to return to the city and her marriage to the warrior prince. Idly she wonders whether she also would wish to remain single if she was able to look at the magic crystals, and whether they would protect her from harm, but she does not think that this is likely. Her life is already protected, and has been mapped out for her. She cannot yet see that there could be other ways, other paths.

She begins to consider ways of killing her friend. She realizes she will miss her and her sisters in the camp. For a while she is very sad. The woman knows why the girl is sad. But she says and does nothing.

One morning the women carrying water from the river find the headless body. It lies upon the pine needles under the great tree. The young princess is missing. There is no sign of a struggle and nothing had been heard in the night. To the throaty murmuring of the doves the women calmly bury their friend and chant their beautiful threnodies over her grave. No one tries to find the missing girl. No one seems surprised.

When the princess, dragging her heavy, bulky burden is still many miles from her city she is met by a messenger. He ascertains that she has indeed carried out her marriage task, and departs at speed to inform his master.

By the time the girl is in sight of the city the armistice has been called and the noisy opposing armies throng and surge through the wide paved city streets and sunlit squares. The feast for the warriors is prepared. Venison sizzles on the roasting spits, the bloody discarded hides and horns lying nearby to be used by the young bucks in mock battle after the banquet. Wives and children are banished to the hills for the night, leaving a troop of prostitutes to serve the food and provide the entertainment. All is ready for the men. In anticipation of the spectacle to come a dais is erected at the centre of the main square.

As for the princess, a room has been prepared in the palace. She is allowed to stay in the city. But she is not allowed to know what happens at the feast. No one really expects her to be troublesome. But in case she is tempted to peep, the wine with her evening meal is heavily drugged.

All is ready now. The cool white walls and towers of the marble palace are warmed and softened by the rosy fingers of the setting sun. Long blue shadows lie slanting across city squares like fallen pillars. Trumpets sound, and the massed voice of the soldiers rises to a jubilant clamour. Here is the prince, ascending the steps of the dais, holding aloft a bulky, heavy-looking bag.

As the frenzy builds to its climax the princess sits in her room, looking with puzzlement at the small phials taken from the pocket of the woman she has killed. They are empty. Inside the phials, little cavities each contain a thin clear fluid. Nothing else. As she peers into these hollows, tiny twin reflections of her own face look back at her. Still closer she peers, and now she sees, not her own reflections, but a sallow bony face, with tawny hooded eyes and wild, wild hair, gazing reproachfully back. Without warning, like the sharp unexpected pain from a knife slash, she is suddenly stricken by anger and remorse. Bitter remorse for the betrayal and murder of the woman who had been more like a mother than her own. Searing anger for those with the power to cause her to do such violence; and anger for herself, who never questioned or challenged this power. Bereft, she sinks to her knees. What can she do now? The door of her room opens and an attendant enters with food and wine. But wait...

Outside, a sudden, stony silence. The princess rises, walks past the attendant with the food, and out across the great square.

As if in a dream she zigzags her way around the still, silent men. Slowly she ascends the wide steps to her warrior prince. He stands, arms stretched upwards in futile triumph. In his petrified grasp hangs the head of Medusa. The eyes are closed at last, keeping their secret for all time. The once wild hair waves serenely around the peaceful face. Thoughtfully, with mild regret, the young princess strokes her warrior's stony flank. With care she removes the head of Medusa from his stiffened fingers and wraps it tenderly in her soft violet cloak.

The dreamlike silence is pierced by the tinkling of little bells which dangle from the ankles of the whores as they trip from the palace, chattering and chirping like a flock of multi-coloured birds released from captivity. Swiftly they strip the golden gem-studded rings and amulets from the immobilised armies, decking themselves in the spoils as they dance and dart about the square. Some of them, in what might be thought to be a rather mercenary fashion, begin to make plans to sell the stone figures to a buyer of artefacts from a neighbouring city. Someone even suggests that they could have an auction in the square, with special reductions for more than five items.

The young princess keeps just one of these statues, for old times' sake. She leaves the city to live by the sea for a while. Sometimes she takes a lover. Sometimes she is alone. Now and then she looks with placid eyes at her stony warrior standing on the seaward terrace.

The younger women of the camp, allowed to live in peace at last, visit her often. They love to listen to her stories!

A Bird

Cath Staincliffe

She ran all the way to the settlement, to tell Martha. She arrived. The tatty little curtain was drawn across the doorway. Martha was out. Her heart swung in disappointment. She dithered for a moment, scuffing the ground with her toe before wheeling off back up the hill to the gully where she'd seen it.

It was a day like any other; hot, dusty, dark and like any other day it had stretched interminably on, a hopeless cause, a length of time to be endured – until her discovery.

She often played in the gully. The mud at the bottom was cool and pleasing to the touch. Ignoring the fetid smell, she'd take off her sandals and push her feet into the smooth, thick paste, leaving little casts from the squeezings between her toes. Or she would wriggle into one of the small caverns and lie sandwiched between the rocks. The coolness pressing along her back, against her skull, the palms of her hands. She drank in the smell of damp, breathed the air deeply, its odours of stone and earth so sweet after the gritty, sulphuric taste of real air. Sometimes, lying prone in her petrified bed, she would deliberately breathe deeper and deeper, down, further down, faster, until her blood sang, her heart crept into her throat and she went spinning into another place, another time, where the colours cracked and danced like hope.

She'd heard it before seeing it. An unfamiliar sound, flapping like wet cloth, chittering, a sound you'd make for a baby. Alarmed at first, she froze, breath shallow, quiet, waiting. Her eye caught movement to the left, down the gully. She turned in time to see it fly, planing across to a stump on the opposite side.

'A bird,' she whispered to herself. For though she'd never seen one the old stories and songs were full of birds. She wondered fleetingly if it might harm her but found no reference in the half-remembered phrases and fragments concerning mocking-birds, blue-birds, blackbirds, geese and nightingales, to any bird killing people.

'Besides,' she reasoned, 'it's so tiny, small as my hand.'

For several minutes she watched the bird. It hopped from here to there, cocked its head to one side, spent some time burrowing its beak in its chest. It flew from one side of the gully to the other time and again. On each occasion she was entranced. To do that, so, to stretch out her arms and soar, to flit from place to place. To fly. She felt a spark of fear each time the bird took flight, that it might go, might fly beyond the gully and away.

She'd tell Martha about it, Martha would believe her, however unlikely the story. If anyone knew how to encourage a bird to stay it would be Martha. Where was she, why did she have to be out now? Now, with a bird to see.

It was Martha people went to with fungi they'd gathered, to check they were safe to eat. It was Martha who'd gone on about the water and sickness and had persisted in building the new well and even heating the water. 'As if everything isn't as hot as hell already', people said though they noticed that Martha didn't get sick and for all her funny ways she could name an illness or explain the meaning of a song better than anyone. It got so people called in on Martha whenever some new thing had to be done. Martha had even grown things. A strange green plant which tasted of nothing and some bitter white roots wich she ground up for drinks and medicines. But most of the time, like everyone else Martha ate what she could find: berries, fungi, small black beetles, wally grubs and dognuts.

As she reached the top of the hill she squatted down to get her breath and listen for the bird. She heard it immediately, chattering and whistling though it couldn't be seen through the dust. She scuffled down on all fours until she was near enough to see it. As she caught its movement she held her breath. The bird circled, dipped, circled again. Chin on her hands she watched for several minutes. Reassured she hoisted herself up and out of the valley and ran back down to Martha's. The curtain was drawn back. She was gasping and wheezing and had to sit for a while before she felt ready to rouse Martha (who had explained time and again that the world wasn't fit to run in any more).

When Martha answered her call she gabbled her story and clamoured to know how to keep the bird here.

'Bird. You've seen a bird. Oh, lovely. A bird won't be kept you know. Certainly not alone. She mightn't stay, but if we give her some food.'

'An' maybe her family'll come too.'

Maybe,' Martha sounded doubtful.

She followed Martha into her home, a dug-out like her own, and waited impatiently while she fished in a corner for seeds and berries to tempt the bird.

'Let's see this bird then.'

Walking back to the gully she was forever running ahead and then back to Martha in loops of excitement. Martha seemed to be taking a lifetime to cover the distance. As they neared the gully she slipped her hand into Martha's and pointed with the other to where she had last seen it. Martha smiled and nodded that they should make their way first along the edge of the ravine. Then she heard the murmur of voices and the grating sound of people scrambling up the rocks in their direction.

Two boys appeared over the lip of the valley. In an instant she saw, knew. Clutch of feathers in the hand of one. Smears of blood around their mouths. Look of guilt succeeded by defiance.

'Got a bird,' he spoke aggressively.

'Not much meat on it,' the other boy shook his fingers free of the bloody feathers.

'Stupid thing.'

They ran off into the dust.

She turned to Martha, tears spilling, anger swelling her throat. She pressed against her, burrowing with her fury and grief. The look of the bird, its flight, delicacy, that chirruping sound. She pulled herself away and looked up at Martha.

'Another one might come...one day?'

Martha sighed, her eyes were dry, lost in the distance, reflecting dust. She turned and walked away down the hill. The clump of feathers lay still, unmoving in the leaden air.

An Old Wives' Tale

Janet Whalen

There were three old wives in a laundrette telling the tale.

'Filthy night out,' one was saying as I wrestled my washing in through the door, soaked from the rain. They stopped talking abruptly when I walked in. Only a whisp of cigarette smoke moved, curling upwards. I could feel six eyes watching me as I inexpertly fumbled with the coin slot and loaded my clothes in, dropping odd socks on the floor. My hands trembled over the soap powder. I laboured to breathe air heavy with moisture and heat. The windows had begun to steam over, sealing us in. I slammed the door of my washing machine in a professional business-like manner. I retired to a corner to recover and got between the pages of my book, trying to merge into the background and pretend I was somewhere else.

I was reading *Macbeth* but couldn't concentrate on the plot because the hubble, bubble, toil and trouble bit seemed to merge in with the boiling, foaming suds simmering round the door of my washing machine. I found myself reading the words in time to the churning of the wash. The machine sounded like it was eating my clothes, chewing them noisily, ready to spit them out, a bad tempered dragon in a boiler suit.

Suddenly, someone else's machine went into a spin with an ear-splitting shriek making me start and drop my book in a puddle. The wives cackled and laughed noisily. I was shaking with nerves, I felt like I was in a torture chamber, a coin-operated torture chamber for which you needed the correct change. I began to feel dampness seeping through my clothes, 'wet rot' I thought sagely and shifted around a bit. I felt like I was being stewed.

The old wives started talking again as the spinning stopped and the weaving started. Outside it was dark, the rain hammered down. One of them spoke in a low incredulous voice as if she hardly dare believe what she was saying.

'Our cat,' she asserted mysteriously, 'has never recovered.'

She emphasized the word 'never' violently and paused for effect. The others were stunned momentarily and then tutted in harmony like castanets.

'Cats know,' said one, by way of explanation.

'Cats know what?' I thought, 'what do cats know?' I very nearly fell off my chair leaning forward straining to catch every word.

'It was on a night like this,' the first one continued, with a voice of doom, 'pitch black it was outside, and rain? You never saw 'owt like it.

'It all began with a trip to Blackpool, I hadn't been for years, I went with Mabel, you know what she's like, she's into everything if you don't watch her. It was her idea we should get our fortunes told by one of them gypsies on the front. I thought it was all a con and told her straight. "Mabel," I said, "you may as well flush your pension down the toilet, you ought to know better at your time of life." She was dead set on it though, she's one of them that'll believe 'owt. She'd had it done before, "It's uncanny," she said, "they'll tell you all about yourself." "Mabel, I already know all about myself," I said. "That's what you think Doris Trusswell," she said in that daft manner she's got, trying to be important, and she was off down the prom like a whippet.

'When it was my turn I pulled back the awning of the tent and stepped in. The air was thick with that smelly candle stuff. Perfumed smog. I wanted to choke. I stepped up to the table fumbling for my fifty pee – you have to cross their palms with silver of course, you don't get 'owt for nowt do you? I was dead septic but I felt a bit feared too, I don't know, maybe I thought she'd tell I didn't believe in her and might take it nasty – you never can tell with some folk. Anyway she studied my palm for ages it seemed and then slowly looked up at me right into my eyes. I felt sick. Her eyes drove into mine like rivets and held them. She had an expression of such unspeakable horror on her face. I'll never forget it.

'It went suddenly ice cold in the tent and I shivered as if a sudden shaft of death had shot into my mind, my disbelief shattered to splinters in an instant, like a dropped icicle. She started shaking her head and drew back afraid, mumbling words of a spell or a prayer. I forgot I didn't believe, I had to know what she'd seen, didn't I?

'She shook her head and said she wouldn't tell, but I'd paid I reminded her. All she would say was that she had seen evil. A figure, she said, shrouded in black, no features were distinguishable in its shadowy aspect and its arm was extended, pointing in a calm barely pent-up, gesture of total violence.

'I couldn't get out of that tent fast enough. To Mabel I wouldn't say a word other than it had been the usual rubbish, didn't want her blabbing everything out to everyone, you know what she's like. I don't remember the journey home at all I was that worried. I tried to shake the memory off but it sat there at the back of my mind like a big black crow.

'A few days later came the storm. Rain drenched the garden and the streets became rivers carrying along tree branches and litter. I was in the house alone. I could hear the weather raging outside, attacking the house and every now and then I could see the sky crack with lightning and the trees wrestling with their branches as if trying to escape from the earth.

'Suddenly I heard three knocks at the door, not the mad pounding of someone deperate to get in out of the storm but calm measured knocks like someone knew I was in there. The cat went beserk, running round the room and trying to hide in the coal scuttle. It knew, you see, knew it was evil. I trembled in my chair spilling my tea over my knitting and turned the wireless off to listen. Silence.

'I decided I wouldn't answer it and just sat shaking in the dark. Then I heard the handle turn slowly and decisively, and heavy boots walk into the kitchen. There was a creak as the door closed. I knew I'd locked the door but that didn't matter at all. All I knew was that whatever it was, it was in the house with me. I couldn't move but sat and watched this figure in ghastly black, materialize right out of the wall. I wanted to scream but couldn't.

'I couldn't see the face at first, it was hidden in the sinister folded shadows of the hood. Its ghastly presence filled the room. All I could do was moan, and in a slow menacing movement, it lifted its arm, and it pointed silently. In the light from the fire I caught a glimpse of a savage, skull-like face and the jaw, like a crooked unoiled hinge, slowly began to open...'

The old woman looked up at me, through the damp air of the laundrette, and saw me listening intently, though I immediately pretended I wasn't.

'Oi! Bugger off!' she said, with a distinct note of indignation in her voice. I started and immediately began checking my washing. I scowled to myself, now I might never know the end of the story. The old woman was nattering away to her companions about eavesdroppers being the scum of the earth. I decided to hit back with a broadside of cynicism.

'Anyway I don't believe in ghosts,' I said decisively and loudly, as I emptied my wash into a drier. '"Ghost" is merely a convenient label for phenomena which appear, miraculously, to defy nature. There's always a logical explanation to be found if you look hard enough. Often it's all in the mind of the victim.'

Smugly, I turned round to find myself alone. I was just in time to catch the last of the three barely visible and clearly engaged in walking through the wall. Almost transparent, she was smirking and waving regally. I was mortified and stood staring at the wall, as an arm reached back through the paintwork and gesticulated rudely at me. I still stared.

'Bloody show-offs,' I thought.

Biographies

Cathy Bolton
I live and work in Manchester. Spend much of my spare time talking about writing and occasionally doing it. I have previously had some poetry published but this is my first short story. I am a great sea-worshipper and lover of day-dreams, as you may have guessed from reading 'Sea Witch'. I have been involved in various writing groups over the last few years, primarily the Outlanders.

Alison Chisholm
I was born in Liverpool in 1952 and educated in Southport and Middlesborough, where I trained to teach speech and drama. I now live in Southport. I am married with two daughters.

I started writing poetry when I was eighteen, and first attempted prose in 1980. My short stories have appeared in various magazines and been broadcast by BBC Radio Merseyside and BBC Radio Network North West. I also write personal experience features, many of which have appeared in the *Dundee Courier and Advertiser*, and articles on the craft of writing for writers' magazines. I have had approximately three hundred poems broadcast or published in magazines, anthologies and collections.

I run a small academy of speech and drama, and teach creative writing in adult education classes. I am poetry tutor to the Southport Arts Centre, I give readings and seminars and adjudicate poetry competitions.

Sylvia Christie
I was born in Aberdeen more years ago than I like to think, and have lived in the North West for twenty-five of them. I work part time as a tutor at Stockport College of Further and Higher Education, and part time for the Workers' Educational Association. And I write, and I keep the family under my thumb, two areas where success is sporadic rather than consistent. However, I have been lucky enough recently to be broadcast on 'Morning Story', and to win one or two prizes in competitions. Not so lucky with the family, who are oddly

resistant to my good offices.

I've just finished a novel, and would like to think that I'll be starting the next one soon – it's still at the stage of scribbles on the backs of envelopes and car park tickets. But in between times, I like to write poetry (got one in Manchester Poets 1990 collection) and short stories. I'm a great fan of science fiction, and have recently discovered Terry Pratchett. But my favourite writers have to be Penelope Lively, A. S. Byatt and E. F. Benson. Why can't I write like that?

Alison Guinane

I was born in Manchester, lived for a time first in Derby then in London, read English at university in York. I began writing when very young but only recently considered a role seriously as a writer, when my stories and poetry began to be accepted for anthologies and magazines. On the whole, I find it easier to construct poetry than prose, I enjoy reading it aloud. I take a keen interest in all the creative arts, teach at a sixth-form college in Manchester and have one daughter away at university. At present I live blissfully alone with two cats, a rabbit and two mice, spending much of my spare time 'scribbling'.

Alrene Hughes

I was born and brought up in Northern Ireland, moved to Manchester in the late sixties and now live in Bury with my husband and two young sons. I have worked in personnel at British Telecom and behind the scenes on live TV at the BBC. I have also spent six very happy years at home looking after my children and studying for a degree with the Open University. In September 1991 I begin a one-year teaching course and after that I hope to teach English.

I started writing about three years ago when I joined a creative writing class and since then I have had short stories broadcast on local radio and published in the Crocus collection *Now Then.*

I am a member of the 'Bury Live Lines' writers' group and have found that the friendship and encouragement of other writers helps with my writing. I also enjoy performing with the group and helping with its workshops.

My short stories usually revolve around relationships and

how the characters perceive the world and their place in it. At present I am doing research for a novel which is set in Belfast during the Second World War.

E. M. Kkoullas

When I wrote this story several years ago I hadn't heard of the so-called 'nuclear winter'. By some oddity the subject cropped up on television just as I'd finished it and I remember the strange sense of *déjà vu*. At the time of writing it had just felt right. Then I was a penniless ex-student living in Hull. Now I live back in my home city of Salford with Boris Karloff and Bela Lugosi, alias the Furry Fiends. I'm twenty-nine and teach in North Manchester. When I find the energy I'll eventually get round to finishing my novel, also science fiction. My first love, though, is the ghost story. Give me something by M. R. James or Francis Marion Crawford and I'm happy. I'm an armchair ghost hunter and a member of the English Civil War Society (I dress up and pretend to be a ghost). Now the thank yous – Robina Hill for the title of this story (Robina where are you now?) and Barbara Watson and her intrepid band of writers who boldly go on Wednesday nights. Finally, my unusual name comes from my Greek Cypriot father and I disclaim all responsibility for it.

Jane McNulty

I was born in Cadishead (was in Lancashire, now in Salford) in 1955: I still live there, with a teenage daughter Katie, three dogs and a long-suffering man called David. Presently, 'taking a career break', I fill my days walking the dogs, trying to shift dog hairs from the furniture, catching up on my reading and running (anything in fact to avoid having to sit down and finish 'the novel'). I am trying to come up with a great way of making enough money to be able to retire to the Languedoc region of southern France but until then I am looking for a job. Two other ambitions are to sing the parts of 'Musetta' in *La Bohème* and 'Anita' in *West Side Story* – although I'm not sure that I can sing at all! I am a Green and am involved in a local campaign which keeps a beady eye on our local toxic waste industry. I also try to avoid growing old gracefully, preferring to do it disgracefully instead.

Thea Parker

I was an only child, born into a middle-class home on the outskirts of Manchester in 1923. Schooldays really were the happiest time of my life, and spent in a semi-detached Victorian house in Withington village. Two elderly spinsters taught thirty or so pupils everything between them, with an accent on good manners and a healthy fear of the wrath of God. I don't remember excelling at anything (except English and composition in which I was always top) but the influence of those two wonderful teachers has stayed with me throughout my life.

At fourteen, when it was legally possible to leave school, my parents sent me off to work in the millinery department of Marshall and Snelgrove's, then in St Ann's Square, in order to augment the family income (albeit only seven shillings and sixpence per week). The hours were long and the work arduous and after three miserable months I persuaded them that it wasn't the life for me, and so began a course of shorthand and typing at Loreburn College.

By the time the Second World War started I had completed my training and soon found my niche in hospital administration at the Royal Infirmary, going on later into hospital social work.

In 1950 I married an ex-RAF pilot and we settled in Cheadle. Two sons, a grandson, and many years of typing later I found myself retired and eager to take up something new, so I enrolled for a course in creative writing, to find to my astonishment that life had come round again full circle and I was back to writing the stories I had so loved doing as a child.

I enjoy writing and reading poems, especially R. H. Davies because of his love of the countryside. Elgar's music makes me cry and Sullivan's can be guaranteed to prise me out of the blackest of moods. If I could choose where to die it would be in Somerset, for there one could not help but believe in heaven.

Sheila Parry

'I write for my life, not for my living'. I can't remember who said that but it's certainly true for me. Maybe one day I shall be able to do both.

My main concern is poetry and I was delighted to have my work published by Crocus books in *She Says*. Writing short stories is a comparatively new and difficult venture for me and it is very encouraging to be included in *Herzone*. It's possible to explore serious and controversial themes in fantasy and science fiction and this is what I've tried to do in 'Till Death Us Do Part'.

From childhood and through marriage, motherhood and a varied career in business and education, writing has always been essential for my sanity in an increasingly complex world. Studying for my degree with the Open University was a turning point – a mind-opening experience which led to significant changes in my personal and professional life.

I'm involved with the local arts scene in Chester as Secretary of Chester Poets and on the Chester Literature Festival Committee. I also enjoy reading, theatre, attending a literature study group, working for Oxfam, cooking, knitting and my Persian cat Muffin.

My two sons are grown up and I now live in a ninth floor flat with wonderful views. I'm happy here and it's the nearest I'll get to an ivory tower.

I'm now working on a collection of poems taking a new look at familiar fairytales and hope to find a publisher soon.

Cath Staincliffe

I live in Manchester with my partner, son and baby daughter. I do freelance cultural projects with community groups.

These are the first stories I've had published. I've always written, mainly poetry, but didn't feel confident enough to show my work to anyone. In 1986 I went to the Womanswrite workshops at Commonword. The regular meetings and supportive atmosphere gave focus and impetus to my writing. In 1988 and 1989 I had some poems published in *She Says* and *No Earthly Reason?* by Crocus books. Recently I've been going to a novel writers' group. Again I've found that structure, support and constructive criticism invaluable.

I grew up watching *Dr Who*, *My Favourite Martian* and *Lost in Space*. Remember the moon walk? As a teenager I read my way through the science fiction section of the local library. I knew virtually anything I picked up would be a 'good read'. And there'd be whole worlds, species, cultures created that shed light on our own. Futures that led me to wonder where the present was taking us, aliens, stars, space travel. Great stuff! It was something I wanted to have a go at.

I currently patronise the crime fiction shelves (will it be

westerns next?). I've recently finished writing my first novel *Murder at the Community Centre.*

My plans for the future are to develop public work as a writer and to embark on another crime novel.

Christine Wainwright

After spending my early years in Yorkshire, then living for a time in Zambia, I settled in Stockport and did three years nurse training. I worked for a while as operating theatre sister at Stockport Infirmary, then feeling a need to change direction, left nursing to do a General Arts degree at Manchester Polytechnic, continuing to study for an MA at Salford University.

At present I still work part time at Stockport Infirmary and teach creative writing for the local education authority and the Workers' Educational Association. My main concerns are my family – a son, daughter and grandson, then writing and painting, walking and music. I enjoy exploring and writing about family relationships, a subject endlessly fascinating, if often disturbing! Drama and short stories interest me most, and at the moment I am working on a play for radio based on an incident which happened this summer whilst staying at Arvon – the writers' centre in West Yorkshire. I would love to write for television, and whilst appreciating the difficulties of breaking into the medium, intend to keep trying!

Janet Whalen

I am twenty-seven years old and live in Withington, Manchester. I was educated in Manchester, Sunderland and Cardiff, and have had a variety of occupations since leaving full-time education including clerical work, cataloguing, computing, sausage roll packing and cleaning. Now, many buckets of detergent later, I work for Manchester University and for the Palace Theatre and I find I prefer this. Besides writing, I am very interested in sport, music, literature and the theatre.

I began writing at school, thousands of years ago at the dawn of time, but began trying to take it 'seriously' about a year ago.

When writing I tend to focus on character above all else, and try to explore and present those I find interesting or admirable in some way. From this point of view I write largely from my own experiences. I also write poetry – usually in an attempt to make sense of things because life is *so* confusing, isn't it?

Pat Winslow

I live in Bolton with eight cats, a bicycle called Edith, and various pot plants – all of which are unnamed and over-watered at the time of writing. My previous occupation prior to taking up the pen three years ago was as an actor and occasionally as a musician. My only real regret is that I never succeeded in distinguishing myself as a bass guitarist. Now, with twelve years acting experience under my belt, I can also lay claim to a first novel. However, I'm sorely tempted to bin it. I seem to have outgrown the original intention. One of the hazards of undertaking a long-term project, I suspect. I find writing poetry far more satisfying. I was published in *Beyond Paradise* (Crocus books) last year and since then have gained in confidence thanks to the Womanswrite workshops at Commonword and the continuing support of my friends.

I also teach creative writing to a group of elderly people in Collyhurst. I've been doing that for a year now and I'm still learning. I've also been running a reminiscence project in Bolton with local residents and a class of top juniors. Very stimulating. And challenging too!

I don't have any plans for the future, though a quiet peaceful life would be very much appreciated – I'm dreading the poll tax bailiffs coming round! I think I'd like to live abroad for a bit. As I'm fairly passionate about cycling, perhaps a spell in France would do me good. A year or two in a tent with the complete works of Colette wouldn't go amiss.

Sue Wright

I can't decide whether it was luck or just sheer talent that led to my first serious attempt at short story writing being published! For whatever reason I am delighted and very proud to see 'Between the Lines' in print (so is my mum!).

From Bradford, I am a twenty-nine year old working-class woman. I belong to a family of comedians, my three brothers could well be a valuable source of inspiration for my writing but mostly remain a source of rabid irritation.

My home I share with Mandy who gave me such confidence to write and listened to my story one hundred and seventy-four times until it jelled!

About Commonword

Commonword is a non-profitmaking community publishing co-operative, producing books by writers in the North West, and supporting and developing their work. In this way Commonword brings new writing to a wide audience.

Over a period of fourteen years Commonword has published poetry, short stories and other forms of creative writing. *Herzone* is the ninth title to be published under the Crocus imprint.

In general, Commonword seeks to encourage the creative writing and publishing of the diverse groups in society who have lacked, or been excluded from, the means of expression through the written word. Working-class writers, black writers, women, and lesbians and gay men all too often fall in this category.

To give writers the opportunity to develop their work in an informal setting, Commonword offers a variety of writers' workshops, such as Womanswrite, the Monday Night Group, and Northern Gay Writers.

Cultureword, which is a part of Commonword, and which acts as a focus for Asian and Afro-Caribbean writers, organizes the Identity writers workshop. Cultureword also co-ordinates 'Identity' magazine, and a writing competition for Black writers.

In addition to writers' workshops and publishing, Commonword offers a manuscript reading service to give constructive criticism, and can give information and advice to writers about facilities in their immediate locality.

Commonword is supported by: the Association of Greater Manchester Authorities, North West Arts and Manchester Education Committee.

The Commonword/Cultureword offices are at Cheetwood House, 21 Newton Street, Manchester M1 1FZ. Our phone number is (061) 236 2773. We would like to hear from you.

Recent Crocus titles

Beyond Paradise
An original collection of poetry that celebrates the vitality of gay and lesbian writing. Provocative, funny and touching, *Beyond Paradise* offers fresh perspectives on life in the '90s – and beyond!
'I promise you, once you've read it, you'll keep coming back for another little glimpse of life in the lesbian and gay lane.' (Scene Out)
'The tragic nature of human existence, the fun and joy of being alive are here...' (Gay Times)
ISBN 0 946745 75 7
Price £4.50 Pbk

Relative to Me...
Short stories on family life. Families can be a source of inspiration – or desperation! The stories in *Relative to Me...* show both, with a wonderful mix of serious and light-hearted writing.
'Relative to Me... proves there's plenty of talent just waiting to burst forth from the region.' (Manchester Metro News)
'Twenty refreshingly original tales.' (The Teacher)
ISBN 0 946745 70 6
Price £3.95 Pbk

No Earthly Reason?
Poetry about green issues – *'This beautiful book is a collection of reflections from the heart.'* (Toyah Willcox)
ISBN 0 946745 65 X
Price £3.50 Pbk

Talkers Through Dream Doors
Fourteen talented Black women write about their lives in this collection of poetry and short stories.
ISBN 0 946745 60 9
Price £3.50 Pbk

Now Then
Poetry and short stories illustrating lifestyles, work and leisure from 1945 to the present day.
ISBN 0 946745 55 2
Price £3.50 Pbk

She Says
Five women writers celebrate the vitality and variety of women's poetry today.
ISBN 0 946745 50 1
Price £2.95 Pbk

Holding Out
Women's lives are portrayed with realism, frankness and fun in this excellent collection of twenty-one short stories.
ISBN 0 946745 30 7
Price £3.50 Pbk

Other titles from Commonword

Black and Priceless, poetry and short stories.
0 946745 45 5, £3.50
Between Mondays, poetry from the Monday Night Group.
0 946745 35 8, £2.50
Identity Magazine, poetry and articles by Asian and Afro-Caribbean writers. £1.00
Liberation Soldier, poetry by Joe Smythe.
0 946745 25 0, £2.50
Poetic Licence, poetry from Greater Manchester.
0 946745 40 4, £2.50
Turning Points, a Northern Gay Writers collection.
0 946745 20 X, £2.95

And coming soon – **Flame**, a dual language book of poetry in Urdu and English, from the North West's Asian communities.
£4.50

ORDER FORM

TITLE	QUANTITY	PRICE	AMOUNT
Herzone		£4.50	
Flame		£4.50	
Beyond Paradise		£4.50	
Relative to Me...		£3.95	
No Earthly Reason?		£3.50	
Talkers Through Dream Doors		£3.50	
Now Then		£3.50	
She Says		£2.95	
Black and Priceless		£3.50	
Holding Out		£3.50	
Identity Magazine		£1.00	
Poetic Licence		£2.50	
Between Mondays		£2.50	
Liberation Soldier		£2.50	
Turning Points		£2.95	

TOTAL _____

Please send a cheque or postal order, made payable to Commonword Ltd, covering the purchase price plus 30p per book postage and packing.

NAME . . . .

ADDRESS . . . .

. . . .

. . . . POSTCODE . . . .

Please return to: Commonword, Cheetwood House, 21 Newton Street, Manchester M1 1FZ.